The Specter Rising

The Ambra Wars
Book One

By
James Aspen

THE SPECTER RISING:
The Ambra Wars Book One

For information and to sign up for my newsletter visit

www.jamesaspenwrites.com

Front Cover Art by: www.bookcoverzone.com

For Ian, thank you for reminding me that I used to be
a dreamer.

Chapter 1.

The calm stillness of space wavered in the moments before the cruiser dropped from hyperspace, its massive gray hull stark against the void. Drive engines appeared, a dozen flickering flashes flickering among the stars. Starfighters streamed from the cruiser's launch bay in tight formation, the squadron gaining speed as they streaked towards Paul Riley's ship. In an instant, he knew he was going to die. He pulsed his distress beacon and faced his doom.

The viewscreen of his small cockpit filled with clusters of starfighters bearing down on him. The dull glow of their ion drives blended with the backdrop of stars, and Paul strained to track their movement. His heart raced, and he knew they'd be on him in moments.

With a flick of his thumb, bright blue icons appeared around the tiny ships on his viewscreen. He gritted his teeth, angled the ship's shields double front, and increased his speed. Retreat wasn't an option. His only chance was to barrel through them and try to strand them in deep space. He'd plow through their formation and have a few seconds to cripple the cruiser's engines before the starfighters locked him into a desperate melee.

Once his attack run was complete, he'd try to hold out against the swarm until reinforcements arrived. He would take as many of the fighters down with him before one inevitably cracked his shields and vaporized him. The reinforcements would have to mop up the rest.

"Here goes nothing," he muttered and switched his torpedoes to single fire.

His thumb pressed the targeting button of his stick, and the computer highlighted the nearest ship with flashing yellow crosshairs. He shifted trajectory directly towards the starfighter and centered it in his sights. Sweat made the stick slick in his hands as he waited for the crosshairs to turn the bright red of a target lock.

"C'mon, c'mon," he whispered, wished his targeting computer could lock on the tiny ships faster. At this distance, the computer had trouble locking onto the sleek ships.

The computer beeped, and the crosshairs flashed red. He instinctively squeezed the trigger and a torpedo shot from below his viewport towards the target with blistering speed. With a quick twist of the stick and another thumb flick, Paul changed course and targeted another fighter in the same tight formation. The crosshairs flashed red, and another torpedo was rocketing towards its target just as the first hit its mark.

Paul's torpedo hit the lead ship dead-center. The fighter broke apart with a quick burst of bright flame that fizzled out almost immediately, the cockpit's atmosphere consumed in a flash.

The second starfighter broke away from the main group, trying to evade Paul's incoming torpedo. The doomed fighter was too late, and the torpedo slammed into its side. The explosion severed the starfighter's wing and sent the ship careening into its neighbor. Both ships fragmented into a swiftly expanding cloud of metal as Paul's computer locked onto the final member of the flight group. Paul squeezed the trigger as the ship broke off the attack and started evasive maneuvers. The torpedo changed trajectory, tracking the fighter's new vector with a sharp curve.

Close enough to make out the distinctive shape of the enemy ship as it pulled away, Paul cursed. The ships were faster than he'd assumed. He barely had time to switch to lasers before his viewport filled with a haze of bright green laser fire splashing against his shields.

He squeezed the trigger reflexively and a quick burst of red laser fire streaked towards the remaining starfighters. A lucky hit sent one ship careened off in wild loops from the formation, spinning out of control after Paul's bolts severed a wing from the fighter. A bright flash caught his eye, his torpedo catching up with its quarry and vaporizing it.

"Only seven to go."

His adrenaline surged as energy bolts pummeled his shields and jerked the ship roughly. He twisted the ship into a snap-roll, evading the incoming fire. The dull flicker of strained energy shields appeared outside his viewport, threatening to collapse.

Paul targeted the next ship in the formation and fired. His red laser bursts mixed with the green bolts streaking towards him as the enemies adjusted their field of fire to match him. Paul ignored his flickering shields and kept pouring his blasts towards the sleek starfighter in his crosshairs.

He grinned when the fighter broke apart in a burst of flame when his blasts hit something critical.

Five down. One more out of the fight. I might make it out of this alive, he thought.

He spun into a roll and pushed the throttle to full, barreling through the hole he had punched into the enemy formation. The remaining six ships darted past, already beginning to veer away to come about behind him.

Paul glanced at the shield readout and paled. His forward shields read 55%, with 25% remaining in the rear. If he hadn't doubled up in the front before his head-on run, he'd be fried.

"I can't handle another beating like that."

With precise, practiced movements, he balanced his shields around the hull at 40% and rerouted power from his lasers into his engines to eke out more speed. Setting torpedoes to dual fire mode, he targeted the engines of the carrier cruiser in the distance. The blue glow of its drive plume was bright against the sea of stars even at fifteen klicks.

The cruiser is already trying to get the mining colony in range of their missiles. I better make this quick, Paul thought.

Anxiety pulsed through him as the red blips of the starfighters on his combat map flipped around and crept towards his ship's position at the center of the map.

It was a race now, one that would last seconds. Long enough for a lock, he hoped, but not enough to give his shields time to recharge. All he could do was hope he could launch before they drew him into an extended battle. As if encouraged by his thoughts, the crosshairs surrounding the cruiser's engines flashed yellow as he finally passed into the range of his targeting computer.

"Just a few more seconds," he whispered, willing the flashing crosshairs to change.

Calm washed over him, and he took deep, steady breaths. His focus narrowed as he placed his finger over the trigger. Nothing mattered except his breath and the ship ahead in the quiet of the void.

The distance between his ship and the cruiser shrank with dizzying speed. Yellow crosshairs pulsed faster. The red blips of the starfighters grew closer on the combat map. His shields recharged to 42% all around. Sweat trickled down Paul's forehead. Every moment seemed an eternity. All flickered at the edge of his awareness.

The crosshairs icon flashed red and his finger squeezed the trigger before his mind registered the lock. Two torpedoes shot from his ship, racing towards their target. He kept the trigger pressed down, launching a second pair of torpedoes as his ship began to jerk from the laser impact from behind. Green streaks of energy flashed past his view, near-hits bright against the black.

He glanced at his readout, watched his shields tick from 40, to 37, and then to 30% within a heartbeat. Fear and instinct told him to break off, to flee, but resolve kept him streaking towards the cruiser. His third set of torpedoes left the launch tubes.

Another volley of laser fire rocked the ship. Out of the corner of his eye he saw his shields drop to 18% then to 3%.

He held his breath, hoping it would not be his last, letting it out with a gush of relief when his final volley left the launch tubes.

His torpedoes away, he jerked the stick back and veered in a sharp vertical vector. Stray shots splashed into his forward shields before he left the starfighters' field of fire.

Spinning wildly, he acted on instinct alone, bobbing and weaving through vectors to keep the fighters from clear shots. He balanced his shields again, left with a dismal 6% coverage around his hull - barely enough to stop a few glancing hits. Rerouting power back into the weapons system, He gripped throttle control tight and did his best to keep his flight pattern as random as possible until his lasers could recharge.

The weapons icon flashed green on his console, and he jerked the throttle to zero and kicked in the reverse thrusters. He gripped the trigger and fired randomly towards the swarm of fighters that rocketed into view, unable to compensate for his sudden loss of forward momentum in time.

By sheer luck, Paul's lasers tore through the hull of a fighter and sent it streaking out of view, damaged but not destroyed. He gunned his throttle again and fired towards a second fighter, relying on sight alone to line up his shot. He let out a whoop of triumph as it exploded. A small burst of fire consumed the atmosphere of the small ship, and a molten cloud of metal shrapnel flew into oblivion. Paul locked his targeting computer onto the third fighter and attempted to match its desperate evasions when a sinking feeling passed over him.

What happened to the other three fighters? Even with his little trick, the remaining starfighters should have torn him to shreds in moments.

He glanced at the combat map. Three starfighters were changing direction from their intercept course with the cruiser and headed back towards his location.

Crap, I can't believe I didn't think of that, he thought. The cruiser moved away from the battle at a steady pace, undamaged. The enemy fighters had intercepted his torpedoes before they could hit the cruiser, or at least enough to keep the remaining from overloading the ship's shields and causing damage.

He overcame his shock in time to see his viewport with a stream of laser fire. In an instant, his weakened shields collapsed. His ship tore apart in a bright flash of light and wail of emergency alerts. He had enough time to take satisfaction in taking out seven other fighters before his ship exploded into vaporized metal.

***

Paul flipped over his joystick in disgust. The cinematic animation of his ship's explosion, accompanied by dramatic music on his computer screen, added insult to injury.

"I can't believe that didn't work," he said. He ran his fingers through his greasy brown hair in frustration. He'd been trying to beat that level of *Galactic Command* for weeks now; it tormented every moment of his free time. His previous attempts to beat it had always ended when the second wave of fighters launched from the cruiser and overwhelmed him. He'd assumed if he crippled the command ship before the wave was launched, he could hold out until reinforcements joined the battle.

Of course, he should have known the game designers would program the AI to intercept torpedoes launched at the cruiser. Paul was becoming more and more convinced that he could only beat the game if he splurged and renewed his multiplayer pass. He'd have to join a guild, or pay for an expensive upgrade package for his ship to beat the game.

"Stupid pay-to-play traps," he grumbled. He loved the game, but he hated the company that designed it to bleed players out of every penny they could. As if paying $50 for a game wasn't enough to begin with.

Paul's knees cracked as he stood up from his desk.

How long have I been playing, anyway?

He glanced at the space shuttle shaped clock hanging on the wall of his small kitchen nook. His eyes widened.

"Crap, I'm late for work!"

The mocking tones of the game music filled Paul's tiny apartment while he stumbled around frantically looking for his shoes and a jacket. He scooped his trusty black zip-up hoodie off his bedroom floor and brushed the dust off.

Good enough. Now where are my shoes? He threw his hoodie on and headed into the main room of his small apartment. He spun around the tiny space that was his living room, kitchen, and - since the door had fallen off the hinges - the bathroom.

"C'mon, where did I leave them!"

The loud fanfare announcing the game restarting finally got to him, and he slammed his laptop screen down to send the machine to sleep. The sudden silence calmed him immediately. He hadn't realized how much the background noise had been beating away at his nerves.

Maybe next time I play I should turn off the lousy in-game music; it might help me keep my cool, he thought. Another flash of frustration shot through him and left his forehead aching with tension. He was already annoyed with himself for losing track of time, but thinking about the damned game infuriated him more.

He was out the door and racing down the stairs when his cellphone vibrated his pocket. Still moving fast, he whipped it out and accepted the call without checking the caller id.

"Hello?" The strain in his voice was worsened by his huffing breath as he raced down the hall.

"Paul, where are you?!" Rachel said.

Damn, I screwed her over! Again.

"I'm almost there, I swear!"

"Right, I bet you're just leaving your apartment," she said.

Paul winced as the door to his apartment building slammed shut behind him. "You're right. I'm just leaving, but I'll be there soon. Cover for me, okay? I swear I'll make it up to you."

Her sigh was loud and slow in his ear. His cheeks burned; he hated disappointing her again.

"Look, it's fine. Just get here before Bryan shows up. He's been looking for an excuse to fire you."

Paul crossed the street and ducked down the alley in a steady jog. Cutting through the park would shed a couple of minutes off. As close as he lived to work, he had no reason to be late. "I'll be there in five minutes, I just have to run through Kinsey Park and cut across Wallace and I'm there."

Her voice softened. "Oh, I didn't know you lived that close. You should be okay. Well, did you beat it?"

"Beat what?" The stench of the seafood restaurant's dumpster in the alley made him gag as he jogged past.

"Th level in *Galactic Command* that always makes you late." Her mocking tone let him know she wasn't mad at him. Not really, anyway.

Paul laughed. "Nope."

"Well, one day you'll be as good as me. Or you'll finally join my guild."

Paul loved that Rachel was even more of a gamer than he was. It was the main reason he was so smitten with her.

A car barreled down the alley at high speed. He leaped out of the way, a gust of wind letting him know he'd narrowly missed a detour to the hospital.

"Watch it!" he yelled, shaking a fist at the driver.

"Uh, I'll just see you soon, okay?"

"Sorry, I almost got hit by a car. I'll be there soon." He hung up and started sprinting.

Paul showed up in the parking lot of Grind Coffee Shop, out of breath but exhilarated from the rush of endorphins from his frantic run. A glance at the parking lot showed he had beaten Bryan to work, and relief washed over him. Bryan took his supervisor job far too seriously for the extra fifty cents an hour the company paid him. Paul ducked into the employee entrance and neglected to clock in. He'd claim he forgot later and have Bryan adjust it. Rachel would cover for him if asked; she might get annoyed with him, but she was a good coworker and would never rat him out.

He hung his hoodie on the peg outside the office door, grabbed a clean apron, and took a deep breath before he pushed open the door to the coffee bar. Rachel shot him a glare from behind the espresso machine. She was steaming milk for a cappuccino, her hair frazzled. She jerked her head toward the line of people at the register without comment.

"I'm sorry, I'm sorry," Paul muttered as he scrambled to the register.

"Yeah, yeah, you owe me big time," she said. Her voice was

more lighthearted than he expected, based on her glare.

He met the eyes of the woman at the counter and smiled his best fake smile. "Hi ma'am, welcome to Grind Coffee. What can I get for you?"

"Don't ma'am me! Don't you know how long I've been waiting?!" The woman's shrill tone made him cringe.

Paul let out a quick sigh. *Yup, another day in paradise.* With some effort, he forced his best customer service smile onto his face.

"I'm sorry for your wait. This cup is on us. Now, what would you like?"

Chapter 2.

"Sorry again for being late," Paul said. The click of the lock latching behind the last customer was a welcome relief.

Rachel didn't look up and kept mopping behind the counter. "It's okay, it had just gotten busy when you showed up."

"Good," he said. His eyes lingered on her.

Even covered in grime from a long, busy shift, he thought she was beautiful. Her curly brown hair was pulled back into a bun, now loose and tattered with locks escaping her band. Her hazel eyes darted back and forth, following the motion of the mop. A hint of her tattooed bicep peaked from beneath the thin t-shirt under her work apron. The first time he saw it, he fell in love instantly. It was a complex myriad of interstellar objects - planets and nebulas swirling together in a wave of color. Strong, smart, and confident, she was everything he wanted in a girlfriend.

But he never could quite get the courage to ask her out.

"Hey, do you mind if I duck out early?" she asked, looking up suddenly. Paul looked away, trying his best not to get caught staring.

"Sure, I'll finish up. I owe you anyway." He struggled to keep his voice as nonchalant as he could, his heart racing. "Got somewhere to be?"

"Oh, you owe me more than that." She shot him a not-so-serious glare and then her eyes flicked away, unable to meet his. "I've got to get home and wash up for a date with Bryan."

It hit him in the gut.

"Bryan? Really?! But... I thought you hated him?"

She shrugged. "He's okay." She locked eyes with him. "Besides, he *asked*. No one else has asked me out for a long time. So... I thought I'd give him a shot."

Great, I was late there, too.

"I'll handle things here. Go. Enjoy your date." He hoped his voice didn't sound as forced as he imagined it did.

Rachel hesitated. He felt her eyes burning into him as he wiped down tables. He ignored her, trying not to show how upset he was. He knew his pain was directed at himself for waiting so long, it wasn't fair for him to take it out on her, anyway. He looked up and flashed his best smile, the one he used on customers all day.

"Go on ahead, I've got this. Have a good time."

She smiled back, and his tension faded. "I'll try. I bet he'll try to drag me to a lame sports bar or something."

He laughed. "Or maybe he'll drag you to that new theme bar on Main St. The one with that makes the servers dress up like 'sexy' nurses."

"Oh god. I hope not," she groaned. She tossed her apron in the hamper, her eyes gleaming as she looked back at him. "See ya tomorrow?"

"Of course. I'll make it on time. I swear."

"Sure you will. I'll call you earlier this time," she said. She waved at him as she walked out the staff door, leaving him with the quiet emptiness of the coffee shop.

***

The stars sparkled above as he left Grind's empty parking lot. The city was quiet save for the faint croaking of tree frogs in Kinsey Park. Things died down pretty quickly in Franklin after 9 pm, like most small towns. There were some bars closer to the college campus, but he didn't like venturing there anymore, even when he was lonely. They were filled with the same crowd having the same conversations they'd been having for years, or new batches of first-year students getting wild with their fake ids.

No, he'd rather take the long way home. He needed the time to think. Maybe he'd figure out why he couldn't ever seem to move towards what he wanted, figure out how he'd gotten to be such a hermit, but he doubted it.

The streets were empty most nights, so he walked in the middle of the street. He wanted a smooth surface ahead so he could marvel at the stars without tripping over cracked and uneven sidewalks. The expansive arm of The Milky Way reached out over the park in the clear night sky. Paul remembered seeing the spiral arm of the galaxy more clearly when he was young, but it wasn't completely hidden by light pollution. Not yet, anyway. Franklin had more growing to do first.

Is anyone watching us out there? he thought. He imagined a young alien on some faraway world, peering at the starry sky with the same sense of wonder. *I wonder if they feel as small and alone as I do.*

He spotted the steady light of Venus, bright as it rose over the tree line. Paul's father had pointed it out to him when he was eight, in one of his rare moments of tender sobriety. He told Paul all about the clouds of poisonous gas spiraling over the planet. His father claimed there could have been life on it too, if it wasn't for the planet's slow rotation. Paul had never really been convinced of the veracity of his father's claim, but he smiled as he remembered hours spent drawing the creatures he imagined on Venus. His version of Venus had neon-colored plants with wavy fronds as tall as buildings. Enormous creatures hid beneath the fronds, behemoths with strange spindly legs way too thin to support their body weight. He wondered what happened to those drawings, the slightly grotesque results of his imagination.

Paul never quite lost that sense of wonder. The feeling boiled up whenever he watched the night sky. Most clear nights, he'd strain his neck staring at the twinkling stars on his walk home. He knew he spent too much time wishing he was among the stars for someone his age, but it was a part of his youth he hoped he never let go of.

For years, he'd begged his father to send him to space camp, but the money was never there. Instead, he worked hard, telling himself he could be an astronaut if he put in the effort. But his grades were always mediocre, and he never thought he could join the Air Force. When he was young, he wanted to be extraordinary, to rocket into space and see a bright world below. By the time Paul was ready for college, he had accepted he was average in every way and settled for community college in his hometown. Now, he settled on making a decent cup of coffee, his biology degree gathering dust on his desk, unhung and unused.

He relished the calm walks home from work; the chance to enjoy the splendor of the cosmos helped him unwind. By the time he got home, Paul was usually feeling better about his situation. He might not be where he dreamed he'd be as a kid, but life was still full of majesty.

The thought comforted Paul as he turned down the alley towards his apartment, and made it all the more disorienting when the street exploded around him.

Chapter 3.

Bright red flashes shot from the dark park and splashed against parked cars and buildings. The flashes melted through metal and ignited gas tanks, showering the street in fire and heat. Paul cowered from the blasts by instinct alone, his mind not quite processing what was happening. He ran towards the alley, red bolts of destructive light vaporizing asphalt all around him.

"Get down, you fool!" a woman shouted behind him.

Paul turned towards the sound of boots clattering on the pavement, rushing towards him, dumbfounded. He got a glimpse of her dark cloak before she slammed into him, running at full speed. The air flew from his lungs as she sent him sprawling to the ground by the alley. Pain clouded his vision as red blasts gouged into the pavement where he had been standing, searing him with molten flecks of stone and tar.

Frozen with terror, and reeling from impact, Paul could barely move. The woman grabbed him and dragged him into the alley, away from the destructive flashes. She pulled his flailing body along the cobblestone and tossed him against the building as if he was a sack of potatoes. She propped him up, gently pressing a hand to his chest to steady him.

"Are you injured, human?" she asked, checking him for burns in a blur of motion.

Human, what...? His eyes widened when he saw the woman

who saved him wasn't a woman at all. At least, not a human one, anyway.

Her dark gray hooded cloak and black jumpsuit hid most of her features, but even under the dull streetlight Paul could see pale grayish purple cheeks peeking from her hood. Her colorful hand poked at his chest and arms as she checked him for injury. Her skin rippled and changed with waves of darker purples and reds that flickered across the surface of her skin rhythmically.

Her bright green eyes were slightly larger than a human's and wider set between the thin bony ridge of her small nose. They flickered with an iridescent glow, catching the light of the alley's streetlamp like a mirror. The shimmer, along with the slender, angular shape of her eyes, gave her a predatory look.

"Don't worry, I'll take care of the Varanul," she growled. Razor sharp canines flashed brightly in the low light.

With a smooth motion, she unclasped her cloak and let it fall to the ground when she stood. Quickly, she drew a small weapon from the holster on her right thigh and held it at the ready. Paul had seen nothing like it, but its exotic shape screamed 'laser gun' to him. Simultaneously, she unsheathed a short but sinister-looking blade from the sheathe behind her left shoulder. The short blade was as black as obsidian and wickedly curved. It reminded Paul of a thicker katana with nasty-looking barbs along the dull edge. She flicked a switch on its hilt and the curved edge of the blade glowed fuchsia with a flickering hum of energy.

The mysterious being glanced around the corner, gave Paul a quick nod, and disappeared with a flurry of movement.

With a few short heartbeats, Paul's entire world had changed. His hands started shaking as his adrenaline wore off and shock set in, his mind racing to understand what was happening.

What the hell is going on?

Loud blasts and bursts of light answered from around the corner, coupled with the peal of metal and rock being blasted to dust. The high pitched blare of blaster fire harmonized with harsh, guttural shouts and wailing, angry gurgles of something in pain to build a horrific scene of chaos in his mind. He cowered away, sliding deeper into the alley, horrified by the imagined horror of what the strange woman was facing.

Seconds later, the sounds of battle subsided. After a moment of silent anxiety, Paul peeked around the corner to see if she had survived, trembling.

The street was dotted with smoking holes and bricks were scattered along the sidewalk where they had fallen from buildings. Dark masses were scattered among the wreckage of burned-out cars, enormous bodies laying in heaps where they had fallen. Some smoldered and smoked, letting off an acrid odor of burned flesh. Others lay in pools of what he assumed was blood, a slowly expanding pool of orange around their gray, scaly bodies.

The street was quiet.

Too quiet.

His skin crawled, and he imagined someone, or something, watching him. He scurried behind the building just as a creature unlike anything he had seen dropped into the alley across from him.

It was vaguely humanoid, but didn't quite stand as upright and was twice as bulky. Even with its hunched over stance, it towered above him. It glared down at him with three sets of eyes that glowed a dull red against its slate gray scales. Its face was elongated and angular, its curves accented by sharp, bony ridges that connected to knots of bony plate on its head.

The thing snarled, its vertical mouth slit opening sideways and revealing a third lower jaw bristling with fangs. The creature's reptilian hiss stirred a primal fear deep in Paul's brain. The creature looked like it could rip him in half. Bulging muscles rippled out beneath shards of matte black metal armor protecting its torso.

"Rath hr'al," the thing said. Its deep voice dismissive and mocking. Paul sensed deep disdain emanating from the creature as it casually lifted a menacing-looking rifle towards him.

A bright flash of fuchsia blurred past the creature and half of its weapon clattered to the cobblestone. The woman appeared between Paul and the creature, small beside its hulking form as she raised her blaster. The beast roared and pummeled her with the sparking remnants of its rifle, sending her flailing back. Her blaster clattered to the ground beside the creature as the woman landed in a heap, her body hitting the ground with a sickening thud. Ripples of dark red flashed across her skin.

The thing kicked her sidearm away and tossed the tattered remains of its own weapon aside. Its roaring challenge deafened Paul and made him want to curl into a tiny ball. The woman scrambled to her feet and repositioned herself between the beast and Paul. She held her glowing blade in a backhanded grip, the bright fuchsia edge of her ebony blade casting a dull glow over her back.

The creature flicked its muscular arms to its side, spreading its fingers wide as short, curved talons sprouted from their tips. It snarled and swiped at her wildly, fueled by rage. Still unsteady from the blow, the woman couldn't avoid the creature's attack. She cried out as its talons sliced across her stomach. She dropped into a roll, narrowly avoiding the second swipe from the creature's other set of vicious claws.

Paul scrambled to his feet and ran from the fighting beings, mind racing. He glanced over his shoulder and saw the woman gracefully recover from her roll. Using her momentum, she sliced the creature's side with a fluid motion before spinning out of reach, sending sprays of orange blood splattering to the cobblestone. The beast tried to track her movement with reckless swipes, but she dodged with a confident ease.

Though the creature was more terrifying, Paul could see the woman was faster and far more skilled than the lumbering beast. Now that she had regained her footing, she seemed unconcerned about the outcome of the brawl. Even the waves of colors rippling across her skin had faded into a steady pulse of blues that portrayed a calm serenity along her skin. Curiosity compelled Paul to stop and watch, feeling secure enough now that he was down the alley.

The creature wailed loudly and swiped at the woman, trying to get in close for a killing slice of its talons, but she was too fast for it. With fluid, dancer-like movements, she slipped away from its grasp and left it with another slice from her blade as she spun and whirled around. It growled and tried to grab her in its arms, but she dropped to her knees and sliced the creature's left leg with a smooth slash. The glowing blade cut through its thick leg and bone like it was thin paper, and the thing let out a guttural howl. She tumbled from the creature's grasp in a smooth roll as it dropped. Its arms still flailed to catch her as it fell, orange blood already pooling around the severed leg twitching on the cobblestone.

The thing hit the ground with a loud plop as she finished her roll and brought her blade around to face it. She paused low to the ground in a combat ready crouch. Her blade dripped with a sickening orange ooze beside her, and its flickering glow illuminated deep purple pulses racing across her skin. The thing wailed and growled as it struggled, refusing to quit trying to slice her even as it lay beaten. She stood and casually stepped from the creature's slow advance. She looked down at it with a grim expression as it struggled along the ground, snarling and swiping at her legs. She spun her blade casually in one hand, her stance confident and cool.

"When will you attack?" she snarled at the creature.

"Rgarh da th'rok," the thing barked at her. Paul didn't understand a word of it, but its defiant tone was clear.

With blinding speed, the woman stepped forward and sliced a clawed hand off the creature with a slash of her blade. The thing howled, but still swiped with its remaining hand.

She jumped away from its flailing easily. Thick drops of orange blood splashed against the alleyway as she set her blade at the ready at her side again.

"When will you attack?" she asked again, voice calmer. "Tell me or your death with be as slow as I can make it."

The thing spat at her and continued its ineffective swatting.

Her shoulders sank, and she muttered something that sounded like a curse. Shaking her head, she casually stepped to the creature, avoiding its good arm with little effort.

"Never mind. I don't have time for this," she growled. With unceremonious precision, the woman crouched and decapitated the snarling thing in a smooth motion. It jerked and thrashed spasmodically for a moment, and then settled down, dead. Her stance wavered as she flicked a switch on the hilt of her blade, and its glowing edge faded to black. She wiped the blood from her blade and sheathed it, staring down at the body grimly.

The alien woman was unsteady as she turned towards Paul. Stumbling into the glow of the streetlight, she scooped up her other weapon. As she placed it back in its holster, Paul saw light blue blood oozing from the talon wound across her stomach. The skin surrounding her wound rippling in dark red waves. A few holes in her clothing also oozed blue, and he realized that she had taken a few blasts from those things' weapons.

She looked up at Paul and her eyes grew wider, in an expression he assumed was surprise. She cocked her head at him. "Why didn't you run, human?"

Paul looked around, realizing he had been standing there watching two creatures battle it out in an alley. He felt his cheeks burn with embarrassment. If she hadn't won, that other one would have torn through him seconds later. The smart thing would have been to run away and never look back. To keep running until he was safely at home at his apartment, where he could pretend it had all been a crazy dream. Instead, he had stood there with his mouth hanging open.

"I don't know," he stammered, searching for something to say as he walked towards her. He said the first thing that came to mind.

"You were amazing!" he shouted. He immediately felt stupid. *Really Paul, that's the best you can do?!*

She looked at the blood oozing over her hand from her stomach. "Not good enough, apparently."

His eyes widened. "I'll go call for help. I'll get you an ambulance!"

She stepped forward frantically and grabbed his hand, pulling him towards her. "No! No authorities, I'll be fine, just...." She paused and looked around quickly before leveling her wide-set green eyes at him. "Do you have a place I can rest awhile?"

Paul looked down at her stomach and paled at the sight of the blue blood oozing between her fingers. "But, you're bleeding bad."

She rolled her eyes at him, a disconcertingly human reaction on a decidedly alien face. "I'm fine, but I'll wrap it up real quick so we can get moving," she said.

She pulled a small packet from a belt pouch. She tore it open and pulled out a thin sheet of sheer material dripping with a gelatinous gel. Unabashedly, she pulled up her shirt. Paul gagged when he saw her wound.

Four deep slashes in her stomach oozed blood and revealed a grisly glimpse into her tissues. Torn blue muscle and the curd-like mass of brown fat drowned in her blue blood. Bright red waves of color rippled out from the wounds on her dull lavender skin. He dry heaved in his mouth a little until she placed the sheet over the wound, the slick gel making the material cling to her skin. She let out an animalistic snarl as she pressed the sheet to her skin and jerked her shirt back down.

"There, that will stop the bleeding." She glanced at the tops of the buildings and the alley's intersection. "We have to move in case there are more Varanul nearby."

"Uh, okay, this way." Paul motioned towards the end of the alley.

"Lead the way, human." She pulled her cloak on, wincing slightly as a dark red pattern flashed across her face again.

He stared at her as she moved down the alley. Signs of the brief battle still smoked around him, and bodies of the creatures scattered the street.

What the hell is happening? he thought, watching the limping alien woman move down the alley with a stoic grace. He shook his head and rushed to catch up.

"You can call me Paul. 'Human' might make you, uh, stand out," he said once he caught up.

She glanced at him and nodded. "Okay, Paul. You may call me Edolit Vyn."

***

They made it within a block of his apartment before the tall woman became too unsteady to walk on her own. Paul had to help her stay upright, draping her arm around his shoulders and putting an arm around her waist. Her muscles rippled against him. Edolit was powerfully built and slightly taller than him, and he could barely handle her well-toned frame leaning down on him heavily.

Plus, he wasn't exactly the weight lifting type.

I need to work out more, he thought, his muscles burning.

He had her stop and lean against a building a few times as the strain of carrying her wore him down. She never complained, but he felt her studying him whenever he had to take a break. He imagined she was thinking about how weak humans were, judging the species by his lack of endurance.

They passed a couple of people out for their nightly walks, and Paul imagined how they looked. A wide-eyed nerd, completely out of his depth, and a tall purple-skinned woman bleeding blue beneath a dark cloak. It baffled him that people didn't give them a second glance, only passed by with a casual smile or nod.

Guess we look like a couple of weird college kids out on the town, he thought.

With great effort, he helped her up the stairs into his apartment.

Paul set her down on his loveseat, and she muttered in pained gratitude. Her skin had lost some of its lavender tone and looked sickly gray. Her eyelids drooped, barely covering her vibrant green eyes.

"Can I clean your wounds?" He didn't know what else to do besides clean the wounds and bandage her up. Edolit hadn't seemed concerned about the severity of her injuries before, but he couldn't just let her bleed.

She nodded with a weak smile and a flash of pale green across her skin. Paul found it disconcerting to see how frail she had become after watching her defeat a group of monstrous creatures alone.

Paul rushed into the bathroom, searching for anything that might be semi-helpful. He cursed his understocked bathroom immediately. As bachelor-pads went, his was more unprepared than most. Hydrogen peroxide and a couple of clean-ish towels was all he could come up with. He didn't even have any Band Aids.

He rushed out to find Edolit in an unconscious heap on his loveseat, her chest rising and falling in the slow, steady cadence of sleep.

Great, now what?

Chapter 4.

What are you? Paul thought as he carefully cleaned Edolit's wounds.

He left the massive stomach wound alone. Ignoring the gory stomach wound, he focused on small slashes and burned holes in her arms and torso instead, trusting her gel bandage would take care of the gash.

Gently, he wiped away her coagulated blood, the sticky cerulean gel clinging to his warm rag. Her blood was strange, but not completely unheard of. He knew of a few animals that had blue blood. Horseshoe crabs. Spiders. Snails. Octopus. He assumed it carried oxygen with copper instead of iron. Paul found he enjoyed thinking about how her biology worked. He'd been avoiding thinking about anything he'd learned with his degree since he'd found no job remotely related to it after college.

Once Edolit's wounds were cleaned, he poured hydrogen peroxide over them. She flinched and stirred while the liquid bubbled in her wounds, but remained unconscious. Rippling waves of various shades of dark red spread along the surface of her lilac skin in quick pulses.

I wonder how her skin does that. And why... His mind pondered the possibilities of what might drive such an evolutionary adaptation, straining a little as he tried to recall his anatomy classes. Camouflage would be an obvious reason, like most of Earth's chromatophores, but the way the pulses spread from her wound sites made him think it was a form of non-verbal communication.

He paused and looked at the bottle of peroxide.

Crap, what if this stuff is poisonous to her? Could those pulses be a warning or pain reaction?

Feeling a little foolish, he screwed the bottle closed and set it aside. He'd better wait until she was awake to ask. Plain soap and water would be enough to clean bacteria anyway, she'd have to heal on her own.

Blood and grime washed from her wounds, he got a good look at the extent of her injuries. He expected to see horrible laser burns and deep gouging tears from shrapnel, but most of her wounds were almost completely healed already.

What the hell...

Looking closer, he could see her flesh was growing back at an extraordinary rate. Grisly tendrils of flesh were growing across her wounds in a webbed patchwork of proliferating tissue. The edges of this new skin glowed faintly, and he thought he saw something moving across the surface, too small to see clearly without a magnifying lens. He quickly checked one of the smaller wounds that he had cleaned earlier and saw that it was completely healed, with no signs of a scar.

"Wow," he whispered. He traced his finger lightly over the soft, fresh skin where the wound had been and watched the myriad of colors ripple through her skin in response to his touch.

A flashing light caught his eye, and he glanced at the metal device embedded in the skin on the inside of her left forearm. The device was a smooth silver metal mounted directly into her skin with soft edges. A screen took up most of its surface, with buttons and slots along its edges. The screen was mostly blank, but had an array of small, multicolored dots along one side blinking in a vaguely familiar pattern. As he stared at the thing, trying to decipher its meaning, another dot appeared next to the other ones.

"Is that a health meter?"

It was exactly like the health bar of dozens of video games

he'd played over the years. He leaned back, staring at the blinking lights. Once again, he became overwhelmed with the burning question that had been plaguing him since Edolit saved him.

What the hell is happening?!

The laser burns and minor scrapes taken care of, Paul peeked at the gel bandage she had put over her stomach wound. The gelatinous sheet still pressed firmly against her skin, and the thin sections of her wound were already knitting themselves back together. They oozed with a clear viscous liquid between the incomplete patchwork of fresh skin, but were no longer bleeding.

Paul relaxed. She might be unconscious, but she wouldn't bleed to death on his couch.

That'd be fun to explain. I swear, officer, this alien was alive when I brought her home. I didn't kill her.

Satisfied that she was out of danger, he poured the bowl of bloody water into the sink and washed his hands. He watched the pale blue blood spiral down the drain with fascination while he scrubbed his hands clean.

Paul walked into his room and pulled the blanket off his bed. He grimaced as he caught a whiff of it - he'd been telling himself that he'd take it to the laundry mat "any day" for weeks now. The woman stirred slightly as he placed the blanket over her, but stayed asleep. He kept his eyes on her as he sat down at his computer desk.

Propping his elbows on his knees and placing his chin in his hands, Paul filled with a growing sense of wonder as he realized the implications. There was an *alien* in his apartment. Between the strange biology and the tech he'd seen, he could think of no other explanation. Unless faeries were real and in some sort of interdimensional battle with terrifying reptilian beasts. But that just seemed far-fetched to him.

Humanity wasn't alone in the universe. Aliens were among us and they had come to Franklin of all places. A town of 79,000 people that survived off of a tiny college, failing mines, and sheer obstinance had attracted cosmic forces somehow. And by pure, dumb luck, he was the one who stumbled upon them.

What is happening?

Paul stayed up and let his imagination run wild, imagining what their ships and worlds looked like. He tried to come up with theories about why those grotesque creatures were chasing her, and what kind of conflict was hitting Earth. His mind buzzed with a myriad of questions and wild scenarios. Exhaustion eventually became more powerful than his curiosity, and he fell asleep in his desk chair watching over a sleeping alien woman.

***

Paul jerked awake. His neck hurt from sleeping sitting up in his chair and drool dripped from a corner of his mouth. He wiped it away quickly and yawned.

"You make strange noises in your sleep, human," Edolit said.

"Sorry, I snore sometimes. How are you feeling?"

"Better. My healing protocol is complete. Thank you for bringing me to your...." She trailed off and her eyes narrowed as she glanced from side to side critically. A flash of dull yellow spread along her neck. "... dwelling and cleaning my wounds. I must get back to my ship."

Paul jumped up with a wave of panic. "Whoa, whoa, hold on, you've got to tell me what's going on."

"No. I do not." Casually, she pulled the gel bandage off of her stomach and tossed it on his counter. There was no sign the wound had been there. She considered the space-ship shaped clock Paul had hanging over his cabinets, cocking her head to the side, her skin pulsing a wave of pale pink.

"But I can help you. I *want* to help you." He wasn't exactly sure how he could help, but whatever it was, he would do it.

Edolit turned and studied him. The emerald green of her wide-set eyes flicked back and forth, reading his expression with an otherworldly gaze. Paul had always found it hard to meet people's eyes directly. Somehow, even though her alien eyes should make him more uncomfortable, he found a resolve deep within him to meet her gaze. He didn't know what lay ahead of him if he stayed with this being, but he knew he'd spend the rest of his life wondering if he didn't get her to explain what was happening.

Her shoulders slumped a little and she exhaled, her skin fading to a duller heather tone.

Was that a sigh? Weariness? he thought, trying to decipher her shifting skin.

"Your world is in danger," she said, finally.

"From those... Varanul? That's what you called them last night, right?"

"Someone has sent them here, yes. They appear to be scouting their last targets before an invasion. I was sent to gather evidence so we can help stop them before they act."

She looked at the panel on her arm and pressed on the screen twice, and sliding her finger in a swiping motion. The air in front of her filled with a star map. Paul recognized it in an instant as the Milky Way, its familiar swirling arms of the galaxy making his inner child grew more excited.

"This is our galaxy," she started, and pressed on her screen again. The stars in a small section changed from white into an array of colors. "These are the systems explored by The Federation, thousands of worlds scattered across hundreds of systems."

As a child, Paul was always flabbergasted whenever he tried to wrap his head around the scope of the galaxy, millions of stars and worlds separated by unfathomable distances. He wasn't remotely surprised the conflict was in a comparatively small corner of the galaxy.

She placed her hands beside the map and spread them wide. The map zoomed in to highlight only the explored area. The map became full of stars and tiny plodding planets in an array of colors. Most of the central systems were green with other colors interspersed more frequently the further from the core they were. He assumed the core Federation worlds were the ones in the center.

Grimly, she pointed to dozens of red worlds on the edges of the sector map. "These red worlds show where we have seen evidence of Varanul scouting parties in the border regions of the Federation. We don't know who is sending them or why."

"Which one is Earth?"

"This one." She pointed to a red system on the map's edge. She pressed her screen again, and the map zoomed onto a familiar map of the solar system, complete with swirling asteroids in a cloud between Mars and Jupiter and a haze of comets and rock of the Oort Cloud. Blinking next to Earth were some numbers.

"What do those mean?"

"That's the date of first system survey, about 12,000 Earth years ago. This is the projected date of invitation into the Federation given current rate of development, about 200 years from now."

"So the Ancient Astronaut theory was correct!" His voice was soft, reverent. He'd always assumed the notion of alien beings influencing the growth of human society to be sensationalist nonsense, but the thought now filled him with quiet awe.

She cocked her head, blue waves spreading over her cheeks. "I'm not familiar with that theory. We've watched your society grow from afar while we explored and mapped your system. We are forbidden to interfere or make direct contact until you are advanced enough to settle other planets. Our civilization wants you to develop your own culture before being exposed to ours. At least, according to Federation guidelines."

"Oh." Paul scratched his head, feeling a little foolish. "But, why are you here now?"

"Our civilization has grown fractured," she said. "Many feel a war is looming. Our government has grown more concerned with internal disputes and ignored worlds outside the core for decades."

"Is that why Earth is in danger?"

"With no one watching the borders, worlds are being exploited by criminals and opportunists among the Federation. Vast, powerful companies pillage worlds of their resources and marauders enslave their peoples within shadows of the law."

"And these, Varanul, are some of them?"

"They're a private army, warriors bred in vats to be

completely loyal to their master. The problem is, we've never been able to discover who they serve. The broad range of their activities makes us think their owner is about to seize the entire border region in a coordinated attack."

"Those things bow down to someone else?" A shiver spread down the base of Paul's neck and burrowed into his spine as he imagined what could control those beasts.

"My group has been trying to figure out who is pulling their strings so we can figure out how to stop them."

"Your group?"

Her skin flashed a deep maroon shade he hadn't seen on her skin before. She growled and spoke with a biting tone. "The Federation would not stop what was happening without indisputable evidence and let our concerns languish in committee hearings. Our leaders suspected whatever group is behind these incursions has reached the deepest levels of government. They started a private group to go where the Federation will not."

He watched her for a moment. She was bristling from talking about the state of things, her skin pulses flashing chaotically with violent waves of maroon. This was more than a noble battle for her. This fight was deeply personal. He hesitated.

"You've lost someone in this, haven't you?," he asked.

Edolit looked up at him, emerald eyes wide and a flash of bright blue bursting along her skin that quickly faded to gray. "I've lost everyone. My entire world was pillaged. Now my crew...," she whispered in a haunted tone. "I've lost one for sure, K'tal. The others are likely dead or captured, too."

"So what now? How can I help?" The room was heavy with Edolit's grief. He could feel it in the air. She leaned against the counter in silence, her hand gripping the tile and waves of red spreading up her forearms. *Is that anger or pain?* he thought.

"I need to get to my ship and get the information I've gathered back to our leadership. They can make the case to the Federation Council to protect Earth and send a guardian force in the meantime."

"Can't you call for reinforcements or extraction?"

"No, our ships can jump between worlds, but messages still

need to pass through real space. There are quantum relays built into the Gates, but they aren't secure. Sending a message could cause the leaders of the Varanul to act before help arrive."

"So where's..."

"Wait, quiet," she snapped. She cocked her head to one side and held up her hand.

"What?"

"Get down!" She pulled Paul behind the couch.

The apartment door exploded under the barrage of close range laser blasts.

"They tracked us," she hissed.

Chapter 5.

"Is there another way out of here?" Edolit's voice was steady despite the chaotic blasts filling the room.

"Just my bedroom window!" Paul shouted over the bursts of blaster fire splintering the door.

She narrowed her eyes at the loveseat shielding them and jerked her head towards his room.

"Get ready to run," she growled.

Edolit pressed against Paul's cheap couch. Her arms tensed, surges of vibrant green pulsed along her bulging muscles. She watched the door splinter apart under the hail of laser blasts until it finally fell from its hinges.

"Now!" she yelled. She pushed the loveseat with a flare of unexpected strength. The loveseat flew towards the doorway, crashed through the battered remains of the door, and lodged itself in the doorframe. With a fluid motion, she pulled out her blaster and shot blindly into the hallway beyond while Paul ran.

The room exploded with return fire, and Paul sensed Edolit hurling through the air behind him. He turned and barely glimpsed Varanul scrambling to remove the couch that blocked their way before he made it into the bedroom. A few stray bolts burned through his "The Truth Is Out There" poster hanging by his bed, nearly taking off his head.

Edolit ran straight through the room to the window. With

shocking strength, she ripped the window from the wall and tossed it to the ground.

"Get out, I'll catch up!" she shouted. She pointed her blaster back towards the bedroom door and fired blindly toward the sounds of snarling creatures in the other room.

The Varanul let out frustrated roars. Paul heard them scrambling for cover as the quick burst of Edolit's fire sent them backing away. Paul's apartment burned as the super-heated blaster bolts ignited the walls and furniture. He gasped when he saw his computer explode with a puff of smoke, hit by a stray bolt. There wasn't much in the apartment he cared about, but seeing the machine destroyed hurt.

"Go!" she growled. Paul overcame his paralysis and scrambled past her onto the fire escape, stumbling down the rusty stairs. The wail of the creatures' return fire was loud behind him. He cringed as blasts shot out the window and splashed against the next building.

Edolit let loose another few shots and then ducked out behind him. She caught up to him on the next landing and grabbed his arm.

"There's no time! Jump!."

"What?!"

The surrounding air exploded with laser blasts coming from his apartment. They burned through the metal of the fire escape, showering them with searing sprays of molten metal. Edolit grabbed him and pulled him over the side.

She wrapped her body around his as they fell the last three stories to the ground, Paul's screams muffled by the laser fire and the rushing wind. Her body shielded him from impact with the lid of the dumpster as they landed with a loud clang. The air flew out of him, but she seemed unaffected. Not missing a beat, she rolled with him off the dumpster onto the ground and landed on her feet. He fell in a heap at her feet and groaned. Pain blurred his vision.

"Come on," she yelled as she pulled him up smoothly and headed down the alley. She shot blindly towards the apartment window as they moved away. Paul glanced back in time to catch a Varanul tumbling from the fire escape and landing with a crash into some trash cans.

Paul ran as fast as he could, barely keeping up with Edolit as the heat of the Varanul's blasts warmed the surrounding air. They burned through the cobblestone of the alley and shards of super-heated stone filled the air. The molten stone clung to him and burned him through his clothing, searing flashes of pain shot through him.

He expected to be torn apart at any moment, to feel a laser blast sear into his back and send him sprawling to the ground. His breath burned in his lungs and muscles cried out in pain as he dashed away, fueled by greater fear than he had ever known. But the blast never came. Within moments they turned the corner and ran into the street beyond, narrowly missing a swerving car. A cluster of pedestrians gawked as they ran by.

Paul slowed, his initial flood of adrenaline spent. The intense protests of his leg muscles filled his mind. His lungs burned and he couldn't get enough air. His heartbeat pounded in his ear, pulsing through his temples and bringing a wave of dizziness over him. He braced against the building's cool brick, his vision filled with a myriad of bright dots as he fought to stay conscious.

Edolit noticed he had fallen behind and appeared at his side as the dots faded. His lungs had finally calmed enough to get air, but he wasn't ready to move again.

"Move, Paul, or you will die!" She pulled at his arm while she pointed her blaster at the edge of the alley behind them, her body tense and skin flashing bright sapphire ripples.

Paul took a deep breath. His head no longer swimming, he thought he could move without passing out, and willed himself forward. *I swear I'm going to work out if I survive this,* he thought, forcing himself to jog. He knew he couldn't manage a full sprint and hoped a jog would be enough.

The loud wail of Edolit's blaster next to him made him jump. He turned to see a Varanul fall into a heap on the cobblestone. Shocked pedestrians screamed and scattered as she pushed Paul harshly.

"Go!" she shouted.

Edolit shot back towards the alley as she gave him a moment

to flee before she caught up.

She kept pace beside him now, not letting him fall behind again. She watched the rooftops and street behind them, ready to blast any beast that showed itself. Around them, startled people scurried from their path, shying from the alien woman with the strange gun and rippling skin.

Blasts rained from the rooftop and the street burst into a chaotic storm. Cars swerved off the road or crashed as drivers reacted to the laser fire streaking from above. Pedestrians ran in all directions, their screams overshadowed by the crashing chaos of explosions, stray blasts igniting the gas tanks of parked cars.

"Turn here," Edolit ordered, pushing him off the main road onto a side street. She spun and fired, and Paul heard a creature's wounded roar. Paul kept running as fast as he could, his lungs starved for air and legs shaking. Pinpoints of light sparkled in the margins of his vision.

Not again, please. Paul's head was swimming, and he felt himself slowing, as much as he tried to keep moving.

Edolit halted and pointed her weapon straight up just as one of the Varanul attempted to jump the gap between buildings. The shot burned into the creature's torso, and it crashed into the building beside her with a sickening splat, landing in a heap. It stirred, struggling to rise, until a second shot from her blaster made it slump to the ground.

Paul was still running when she caught up to him half a block away.

"We're okay now, I got the last of them," she said. Screams and car horns echoed from the main street, but there was no more weapons fire.

Paul lurched to a stop and leaned down, propping his hands onto his thighs as he hunched over. He was dizzy again and swayed a little on his feet. He put his head between his legs and tried to catch his breath. Edolit scanned the area, weapon at the ready, but more relaxed. Paul thought it strange that she didn't seem to be winded at all. Her skin pulsed a steady, calm rhythm. Watching her more closely, he could see she was less unaffected than she seemed, her muscles twitching beneath her lilac skin.

"How did they find us?" he asked. He stood up straight and placed his hands above his head to open his lungs, ignoring the sweat pouring down his face. *Yep, definitely need to work out.*

"They must have cleaned up the battle site from yesterday and found my blood. Wouldn't have been hard to track it back to your dwelling," she said.

Paul remembered his computer exploding in a hail of laser blasts and his brand new loveseat catching on fire. Besides his computer, he couldn't think of much of anything in his entire apartment he would miss. Was his life really so empty that he had nothing to lose? The thought struck him deep in the chest.

He hoped the other residents got out before the fire spread out of control. The rent was cheap, and the building was full of poor families and elderly who had much more to lose than him. Guilt hit him as sirens sounded in the distance, still a few minutes away. He wondered how many people were injured on the street.

"What do we do now?" he asked.

She studied him, her vibrant eyes impossible for him to read and skin pulsing clashing tones. Paul thought she looked sad. Or hesitant. Something was going through her head, and not being able to decipher her expressions and skin signals was making him uncomfortable. It was as if she was having a silent argument with herself, the way her expressions flickered.

With a nod and a bright flash of green along her cheeks, she seemed to reach a decision.

"You are no longer safe here, Paul," Her voice was solemn, quiet. "The Varanul likely think you are a Resistance agent now, and will attempt to eliminate you. You must come with me to my ship."

"Me? But I know nothing about this! What would they want with me?" His voice cracked, and he felt like an awkward teenager again.

"They don't know that." She stepped closer and holstered her weapon. "They will do anything to protect their plan. The best I can do for you is get you somewhere far away before I leave your planet."

Paul looked at the Varanul's smoking body and shuddered. The image of people running away popped into his mind, people who had witnessed the Varanul chasing them through the streets. "What about the people who saw everything? Will they be hunted, too?"

Edolit put her hand on his shoulder gently and leveled her eyes with his. "The Varanul's controllers will feed them a lie, most likely through your planet's leaders. Enough will believe the lie to make it fade away. Humanity is not ready to accept the truth, and whoever controls the Varanul knows that. But you have been seen with me. They will assume you to be a threat and hunt you. This city is too small to hide from them."

Paul nodded. He knew too well how small Franklin was. Most days, he ran across a dozen people who knew him. He never thought of himself as popular, but lack of anonymity was part of growing up in small places. There was nowhere to hide in a town like that.

"Okay, I'll come with you. Now what do we do?" He was overwhelmed. His entire being screamed for him to run, but what other option was there?

Edolit pat his shoulder. "Now, we've got to get to my ship before the Varanul find it."

She pressed the screen on her arm and a small map of the city sprung to life in between them. He assumed the small flashing dot just off the main street showed their location. She glanced at it and seemed to get her bearings. She closed the map with a swipe of her hand.

"This way." She motioned away from the main road. "Pay attention for anything out of the ordinary. You might spot an ambush before I do."

"Great."

Edolit glanced down and seemed to realize she no longer had her cloak. Her lilac skin was brighter in the sunlight than it was in the dim light he'd seen it in the night before. She'd be easy to spot in any crowds, especially with a blade strapped to her shoulder and a blaster on her thigh.

"And let me know if we're getting close to a crowded area, I don't want to put anyone else in danger."

Edolit didn't wait for his reply before she moved away. Paul gulped and followed her down the street.

Chapter 6.

Edolit peered around the stone building and muttered something that sound like a curse. She pushed Paul back down the alley, away from the courtyard. They slunk to the end of the block and hid behind a dumpster. A low growl vibrated in her throat and her skin flushed a deep indigo. Paul wondered if the color meant irritation.

She pressed her screen and a small picture of the area popped into view between them.

"They found my ship," she whispered, pointing to red figures on the rooftops of the buildings surrounding the old factory courtyard.

"I saw nothing there," Paul whispered, pointing to the strange wedge shape in the middle of the courtyard.

"My ship's cloak shield is engaged. Trust me, it's there. Nian, switch to tactical view and overlay projected enemy fields of fire," she said.

"Who's Nian?"

"My Ambra," she said. She raised her left arm and pointed to the device on her forearm. "Your people would call it artificial intelligence."

The image shifted to an aerial view of the area, with yellow triangles emitting from each Varanul. Almost the entire courtyard was now yellow except for slivers along buildings.

"Ka'ilk," she muttered in a low growl. Paul didn't need to

understand the words to recognize a curse.

"That bad, huh?" He hoped she couldn't see how badly his hands were shaking in the low light. He was terrified, but letting her know how bad seemed like it would make it worse.

"They have all access points covered, and more have to be on their way," she said. She motioned for him to follow her to the dilapidated old building further away from the courtyard the ship was parked in.

Paul always wanted to explore the abandoned factory outside town, but had never gotten around to it. As they slipped through the gaping hole in the side of the old factory office, what had once seemed like an exciting prospect was now terrifying. The roof had rotted away long ago and the ceiling sagged, threatening to collapse at any moment. The musty smell of mold overwhelming his senses. Remnants of an abandoned vagrant's camp added to the gloom of the building. The place was so far gone, people on the fringe of society no longer bothered to use it.

Edolit took him to the backroom and took a small glowing rod from her utility belt. The pale green glow it cast over the room did nothing to change how creepy the place was. Then she exhaled sharply and pulsed her disappointed heather tone.

"I didn't want to do this, but we don't have many options," she said. Her voice was mournful as she fumbled with a small leather case on her belt.

"Do what?"

Edolit pulled out a small, flat piece of metal, identical to the one embedded in her forearm. This device was stained with dark carbon scoring across the backside and chips gouged in the metal around the screen. She held it out to him reverently.

"This was K'tal's Ambra. I retrieved it from his body before the Varanul chased me toward you last night. I need you to put it on, or you don't have a chance."

Paul took it from her carefully. It was lighter than he guessed it would be, not much heavier than his cell phone. "What is it?"

"The Ambra is an experimental combat enhancer and artificial intelligence. The AI directly interfaces with your neural pathways and musculoskeletal system. It will enhance all of your senses, reflexes, strength, and stamina. It will also heal you from most wounds using nanotech, but you already saw that part." She pointed to the slashes in her jumpsuit from her stomach wounds from the night before.

He stared at her, not believing what he was hearing. "How could that device do all those things?"

She ignored him and continued. "The AI has access to the Federation complete knowledge databanks, access codes for communications relays, and locations of all hyper-Gate points. This one has a copy of all the scouting data we collected about the Varanul's movements in this system. If I don't make it, I need you to get this data to my base. The AI will help you get there. My superiors need to know the Varanul's controller is about to claim Earth, so they can stop it."

Paul's mind was swimming, grappling with an overload of information he didn't completely understand. He stared down at the alien device in his hands, a gateway to an entire galaxy of information and power. The secrets of an alien culture, unfathomable to him mere hours before, nestled in the palm of his hand.

"Why are you giving me this?" he whispered. A heavy weight pressed on him.

"Because there is no one else. I need you to join us, Paul. Your world needs you." Edolit placed a comforting hand on his shoulder.

"But I'm just an average, normal guy. I'm not special. What makes you think I can help?" He wanted to let the device drop to the floor and run, Varanul be damned.

She looked at him coolly and held out her arm, showing him her Ambra. "Because. I wasn't special either when I got this. It saved me, and it might save you."

He looked at her skeptically.

"The choice is yours. I can't make it for you. For what it's worth, I would rather give this power to an average being who is good than see it with someone who would use it for personal gain."

Paul wanted to run. He wanted to disappear and pretend

none of this had ever happened. A familiar sense of panic welled up his throat. The one he experienced any time he had considered talking to Rachel or standing up to his father. The one that made crowded parties and nights at the club a special brand of torture for years.

Joining a group of aliens fighting to protect Earth and dozens of other worlds wasn't what he had in mind when he daydreamed about leaving Franklin. He had imagined working at a coffee shop in a small beach town or something, not charging into battle against a foe he didn't understand.

"This is crazy. I shouldn't be here," he muttered. His hand was shaking. The Ambra was icy against his palm.

"Neither should I. I should be running through the Fields of Hali with my family, but they're gone. The fields. My family. Everything and everyone on my world. Gone," she growled. Her skin rippled waves of blood red. "They will do the same to your world. Soon. They are almost ready to strike. This will give you a fighting chance to change it."

Paul looked at Edolit's face and deflated, shoulders falling with his resigned sigh. He didn't have much choice, it seemed; run and be hunted, or stand and fight. He handed the Ambra back to her with a slight nod. He'd at least give himself the best chance to survive. Maybe he'd be able to help along the way. "Okay, what do I need to do?"

Chapter 7.

"These will anchor the Ambra to you, attach it to your bone." Edolit pointed to the large needles on the underside of the Ambra. She shifted and pointed to smaller fibers, like delicate fibrous hairs. "These will integrate into your systems, nerves, and muscles."

"Sounds... uncomfortable." Paul wasn't excited about an alien device boring into his bones. Not even a little.

"It is alarming, especially at first. Most of ours get installed under sedation. Unfortunately, we do not have that option for you should you choose this path."

"Will it hurt?"

"At first, but after the first probe injects you, it will feel like a burning sensation until it bonds with your nerves. After that, the AI will block your pain response for the remainder of the bonding. It will be disturbing more than painful, especially when it speaks to you."

"What, like, in my head?"

She nodded.

"Okay, an alien AI voice in my head. Got it. Anything else I should know?"

Paul was being testy, but he got that way when he was nervous. And what could be more nerve wrecking than bonding with alien technology? The image of a Varanul flashed in his head, staring at him with its six red eyes and jaws gnashing, only made him keyed up more.

"Well, K'tal had a strange sense of humor, and preferred his Ambra to have the same. His AI was hard to handle." She flashed a brief wave of green to match her amused smile.

"Great, so I'll have a crazy voice in my head, and intergalactic warriors hunting me. Wonderful."

"When we make it back to base, we can trade it for a fresh one and you can choose your own AI. For now, Zyp will help you do your part to aid our escape. If we get separated, it will help you survive. Zyp just might, well, give you a hard time about it."

"Zyp? What kind of name is that for a high-tech AI?"

Edolit's wistful smile was as mournful as deep blue lines on her forehead. "The kind K'tal would've loved. The choice is yours. I won't force you to wear it, but it will help you survive."

Paul looked at the thin metal; there was no going back if he put it on. Part of him wondered if he could run, but deep down he knew it wasn't a choice. Not anymore. Mostly he was more interested in how such a small thing could give him abilities like hers.

"Let's do it," Paul said.

Edolit's skin flashed a shade he hadn't seen before, a pale teal color that faded quickly. Respect, maybe? He hoped so.

"Okay, lay down in case you lose consciousness. I'll place it for you. Which arm?"

"Left," he said, figuring it belonged on his non-dominant hand so he wouldn't fumble with the screen as much.

Paul laid flat with his arm outstretched as Edolit took a small sleeve from her belt and ripped its package open. She took a small piece of thin material from the sleeve, dripping with the same viscous fluid as her medical pack. He assumed it was some sort of antiseptic or healing gel. She rubbed it over his forearm and it wiped away the thin layer of grime covering his skin. The gel numbed his skin to her touch slightly. She placed the Ambra on his arm and he jerked away with a flash of panic.

She smiled. "I'm just lining it up, it won't hurt yet."

Paul relaxed. "Right. I knew that."

Edolit pulsed a wave of green and gave him a side-eyed glance before she went back to moving the device along his arm. He expected to feel the metal sliding across his skin, but no sensation registered.

I wonder how deep that numbing gel goes? he thought.

Edolit looked at the Ambra critically after she had placed it and pulsed green. "Perfect. Okay, this will hurt, but it'll pass soon. Hold still as long as possible."

Before he could reply, she pressed the screen, and the device turned on. He froze, and panic coursed through him. The screen glowed to life with a strange emblem in the middle and flashed into a loading screen. A series of glyphs that looked like random slashes flashed and began disappearing one by one as they counted down.

Then the pain started.

Spikes shot into his skin and he tried not to cry out, but failed with a yelp. The sharp pain subsided as the thing cut deeper into him. A burning sensation traveled up his arm, and he imagined metallic tendrils creeping up his nerves and along his muscles. The image made a surge of animal fear overtake him, and he tried to get up.

Edolit gently pressed his chest and caught his panicked eyes. Her skin pulsing a serene cerulean blue, like the clearest spring sky. "Calm. Breath deep. It will be over soon..."

The burning sensation continued to spiral its way over his bicep and into his armpit. It split into a dozen directions from there, swirling over his chest and back. It seared its way along his clavicle and between the bones of his neck. The pain became a searing burst of light in his vision, and then he was plunged into darkness.

***

Paul regained conscious with a jerk and trashed around in panic, but the pain was gone. Not even a lingering ache where the Ambra had cut into him. His arm seemed slightly heavier, the weight of the device embedded in his arm just enough to be noticeable.

Edolit kneeled next to him. "Better now?"

He pulled himself into a seated position and rubbed his

neck, where the pain had been most excruciating. "Yeah, I'm okay now. I think."

"Good. Voice command override code: 1127."

Bright green text flashed in his vision.

[Command Override Acknowledged. Training Mode Engaged.]

Paul looked at Edolit in surprise. He started to ask a question and trailed off instead. Hovering in the air beside her was a small icon and bright green text.

[Commander Edolit Vyn: Level 10 Scout. Threat Level 7. Display full bio?]

"What the hell?" he muttered.

He noticed another icon in the center of his vision, a small bar blinking across his vision, like a load bar for a computer game. Beneath the bar small green text said: [INITIAL ASSESSMENT SCAN.]

"I assume the Heads Up Display is working based on your baffled expression," Edolit said.

"What the..."

"The HUD is disorienting at first, but you get used to it. Now, if you press this button, you can turn off the display and your AI will only interact with you verbally. You can also give it mental or verbal instructions if you can't move your hands."

"Okay..."

"You will be able to program shut off and start up commands so you can have some privacy once your assessment is done. It can get exhausting to have something reading your thoughts in real time. We all need privacy sometimes." She stood up and held out her hand, and helped him to his feet. "How do you feel?"

"Okay, I guess. Now it is just telling me how dangerous you are and that it is doing an INITIAL ASSESSMENT SCAN."

"The Ambra is checking your physical fitness, skill set, memories, and mental capacity to get a baseline for you," she said.

A loud voice chimed in, and Paul jumped. *Yeah, and it'll take me less time if you stop asking stupid questions, human.*

Paul looked for the source of the voice. "Who was that?!"

She can't hear me, bub. I'm Zyp and I'm in your head now. Lucky me, the voice said with a distinct grumble. *Now calm down so I can work or I'll knock you down a peg on your intelligence score.*

Edolit's skin pulsed a vibrant green, her eyes gleaming. "That would be Zyp. It'll threaten to mess with your scores but it can't. I'll give you a little time to get acquainted."

Whatever, I can do what I want... well, except speak in a language that actually makes sense. How many contradictions does yours have? Thanks for that. Oh nevermind, you learned a little French in high school, now I can speak two nonsensical languages. Didn't they teach you people anything useful, like Chuluthian or Adanomian? What kind of backwater world are we on, anyway?

"Adanomian?" Paul looked at Edolit, stupefied.

"If Zyp wears you out, remember, it's only temporary until you set your voice commands. Also, you don't have to speak, he can hear your thoughts."

Damn right I can.

"Great," Paul muttered. His head was spinning, and it wasn't only because there was another consciousness bouncing around it.

"I'll go keep watch. We'll wait until dark to make our move so we'll have more cover. You'll need time to adjust to your new friend, anyway. Do some exercises to get used to augmentation, I don't want you stumbling out there."

You might get used to me, but I doubt I'll ever get used to being stuck in your underdeveloped mind, Zyp said.

Shut up, Zyp. Paul thought.

Make me. Oh wait, you haven't learned how yet.

Paul was already regretting his decision to take the Ambra.

***

Paul's entire body seemed different. It pulsed with an electric tingle, bristling with extra awareness and energy. He felt a strange distance from his movements, like his consciousness was a passenger in someone else's body. Zyp assured him the sensation was normal, with only minimal mockery. The AI explained it was just his brain trying to process the heightened sensory input and energy efficiency. Zyp assured him his brain would adapt.

Moving took less energy. His stamina could handle cardio exercises with ease, and even in the cramped, dilapidated office he'd been able to tell that it made him faster. He was stronger, picking up fallen bits of rafters from the ground like they were sheets of paper, and tossed them aside with a loud crash. Paul worried that the whole building was going to come down around him until Zyp assured him it was only his heightened sense of hearing.

Paul didn't believe him until he heard the chattering of a mouse creeping in the shadows a dozen yards away and nearly bolted away, thinking it was a Varanul coming for them.

The heightened senses would take some getting used to, but he knew his brain would adjust. Even the softest breeze sent a burst of information coursing into him. He didn't want to think about how bad the smell in the office was. The sooner he got used to his abilities, the sooner he could get the hell out of its stench.

His movements were jerky and awkward, like that of a toddler as he slowly relearned balance and gait. Over-exaggerated and clumsy, he bumbled around until he figured out how to walk without toppling over. Paul had expected Zyp to mock him the entire time, but the Ambra was strangely comforting through the entire ordeal. Zyp assured him that his brain would adapt to "not being a frail weenie," but otherwise it gave helpful advice on how to moderate his movements.

After a half-hour, he was positive he could function semi-normally, and joined Edolit at her perch at the front of the building.

Her eyes were indecipherable as she appraised him while he strode up to her. He was self-conscious, especially as her indecipherable expressions rippled along her skin. His stride was a little stilted, but he thought he was doing okay overall.

"More comfortable with the Ambra?" She asked, turning

back to looking out the crack in the wall.

"Yeah, I'm okay. It's weird, but I'm getting used to it," Paul said.

I'm not the weird one here, sport, Zyp spat.

Shut up, at least I don't talk like a daytime sitcom grandpa, Paul thought back.

Oh good, I was beginning to think you wouldn't fight back. Zyp sounded relieved.

Paul sighed and ignored the Ambra. He might be getting used to walking, but it would be awhile before he was used to Zyp.

"Good, because we need to move soon. We need to reclaim the ship," Edolit said.

"Okay, what do you need me to do?"

She pressed her Ambra screen, and the courtyard appeared in front of her.

"We'll approach from this side, there are more blind spots. You will wait here for my signal," Edolit said, pointing to the edge of a building by the courtyard on her combat map.

"And where will you be?"

"Slitting the throat of this sniper." She pointed to the red figure on top of the same building. The yellow triangle emitting from the point disappeared, and a gap appeared in the courtyard, extending almost to the ship.

He understood now. She would clear the path to the ship, he would get it ready for her to join him.

"How long will I have to get inside?"

"Seconds," she said. She pointed to another sniper on the next building. "If all goes well, I'll be able to neutralize this one as well. You will be completely out of firing range from the rest. At least until they reposition."

"How will I get into the ship and get it started? I know nothing about it."

"The entry hatch will automatically recognize K'tal's access codes in your Ambra and open when you get to it. Once inside, follow Zyp's instructions to get the ship's startup cycle going."

"Okay, got it. How long until you get onboard?"

She glanced at him and he saw something change about her expression. Her skin flashed a mixture of violet and rose in a swirling pattern he hadn't seen before. He wasn't used to reading her yet, but it didn't seem good.

"I'll be right behind you," she said. Her tone wasn't as convincing as he guessed she intended it to be. Before he could react, she closed the map and motioned for him to follow. "Okay, let's get this over with."

It was disorienting for him to not have to struggle to keep up with her, but experiencing his body working at its peak performance was exhilarating as he rushed to catch up effortlessly.

Chapter 8.

Paul crouched in position, waiting for Edolit's signal. He couldn't believe how well he could see in the dark with the Ambra's help. Even in moonless black of the courtyard he could make out the Varanul's movements as they rustled uncomfortably in their lookout points. When he concentrated, he could make out the raspy heaving of their breath among the eerie stillness of quiet. Down the alley, he saw rats creeping in the shadows and heard roaches scampering along the cracks in the pavement.

The only thing he couldn't see was the ship, hidden behind its cloaking field.

Zyp, display the ship's location, he thought. It was strange to give commands to something in his own head. He wondered how long it would take to get used to.

No problem, Zyp said.

An array of geometric lines appeared in the courtyard outlining a ship about 30 meters long. The ship was a sleek, wedge-shaped design with a low profile, resting on three landing struts. Judging by the size of the viewport near the snub-nosed point of the wedge, there would be room for two crew in the cockpit. The larger rear section of the vessel was big enough for a small group of soldiers or stacks of cargo, he imagined. He saw some weapons under the wings and a duel laser cannon mounted above the cargo hold. Paul wished he could see the ship uncloaked, but he had more important things to worry about than what color the alien ship was painted.

Now show me my path, he ordered.

A yellow band appeared superimposed along the ground ahead, moving at an angle away from the sniper's field of view and moving straight for the ship.

He braced himself against the building and waited for Edolit's signal.

And waited.

The seconds ticked by agonizingly slow, giving his mind too much freedom to imagine the worst. *She'd been discovered. A patrol will find me.*

Chill out, Paul. She's fine. Take a breath, Zyp said.

Easy for you to say, you don't breathe.

Sure I do. See?

Paul's chest expand and contract rapidly in an unnatural rhythm that made him feel like he was hyperventilating.

Stop it, Zyp!

Just keeping you distracted. I promise it's for your own good. Okay, take a deep breath. She's about to engage.

Paul got ready to run. Despite his annoyance, he had to admit that Zyp's distraction had helped snap him out of his negative thought loop. His enhanced hearing picked up the sickening sound of her humming blade slicing through the sniper's throat and the bubbling gurgle of its death rattle. His heart raced as he expected the courtyard to burst into laser fire.

The sound of Edolit's voice transmitted by the Ambra into his left ear made him jump. "Go now."

Adrenaline rushed through him when he sprung from his crouch and ran. He broke right, staying inside the path Zyp had laid out before him. There was no time to be disoriented by the projection; he was too busy running faster than ever before. Before he had registered just how fast he was running, he reached the pivot point and overshot it. He stumbled as he tried to turn back onto the safe path too quickly, but recovered. He gritted his teeth and looked towards the ship outline.

A green icon flashed next to the ship's hull.

[*The Specter: Sabre-class* Scout Transport. Threat Level 4. Distance: 100 meters. Display technical readout?]

He ran for the entry hatch and got a rush of satisfaction when he saw how fast the distance to the ship was shrinking. It had only been a few heartbeats, but he was closing fast, and he wasn't even winded. The cool breeze felt amazing as it wafted through his short hair.

Paul was halfway to the ship when the shooting started, loud blasts that made him imagine fireworks exploding right next to his body.

Edolit's voice was loud in his ear, even over the loud bolts of energy exploding concrete and brick. "Ka'ilk. They spotted me. Get to the ship, now!"

***

Combat Noise Dampening engaged, volume set at 25%, Zyp said. Instantaneously, the noise of the laser blasts became bearable.

Thanks Zyp.

Paul glanced back to see Edolit's bright green outline superimposed behind a small chimney. Towards the front of the building, a Varanul was firing wildly at her, blowing bits of brick from her quickly shrinking cover. Bright bolts angled towards her from two other roofs across the courtyard, and Paul could see more Varanul moving along the other rooftops to flank her.

She was pinned down, and all he could do was keep running.

The hatch opened on the ship's side with a snap and rush of air, folded down into a ramp as he approached. He paused at the base and turned as a blaster bolt splash against the side of the ship near his head. He scrambled up the ramp, ducking for cover.

Get to the cockpit, Zyp ordered, its tone even.

Paul turned at the top of the ramp and ran up a small corridor. The cockpit door slid open as he approached and he bounded through it, nearly flipping over the back of a seat. He scrambled to a stop and looked at the two seats in confusion.

Left seat is the pilot's.

He scrambled into the seat. It was big for him, but he could reach all the controls comfortably.

Center console, flip the large switch.

Paul flipped the switch, and various instruments and screens in the cockpit flashed to life with soft lights. Without a moment's hesitation, Zyp continued to spit out commands.

Red button, center console.

Paul pressed it, and a dull vibration rattled the ship.

Left panel, yellow button.

Paul looked down to his left and pressed the button on the panel beside his seat. A soft hum filled the ship.

Top panel, top switch.

Paul flicked the switch, and the metal panels blocking the viewport slid apart from the center. He saw the battle outside clearly, and it had gotten more intense. More Varanul joined the sharpshooters trying to pin down Edolit on the roof, and a small cluster was running towards the ship. Faint red outlines appeared around them in his vision as they approached. He didn't take the time to read the text displayed by each one.

Probably more threat and distance data, he decided, and ignored it.

"Close the hatch, they are trying to take the ship!" Edolit's voice was tense in his ear.

Center Panel, bottom switch.

Paul reached for the switch and then hesitated.

"What about you?," he asked.

"Close it, now!," she shouted, the high-pitched wail of her blaster loud in his ear.

He hit the switch, and the whirring of the hatch closing filled the rear of the ship. The blasts and explosions from outside became muffled by the ship's hull. The sudden quiet was an eerie contrast to the chaos he saw outside the viewport.

The cluster of Varanul roared in frustration, firing at the ship. The cockpit shook slightly as the blasts splashed against the hull.

Shields Up! Left panel, green button.

Paul was getting flustered and couldn't keep up. He looked at the array of buttons and couldn't figure out which one Zyp meant.

This one, genius. A bright arrow appeared, pointing to a button.

Paul hit the button and a faint shimmer passed across the viewport. The Varanul's energy bolts dissipated a few centimeters from the hull and left a faint glow in the air as the shield absorbed and redirected the energy.

Top Panel, Right Switch.

Paul flipped the switch down, and the viewport heads up display activated with various gages and meters he didn't understand.

"Paul, you need to launch. I won't make it to you." Edolit's voice was grim in his ear.

"Wait, what? No, we can do this! I can pick you up on the roof," he said.

"Zyp, scan for hostiles, we've got three ships coming in. If you don't go now, you won't get out."

Top Panel, Left Switch. Zyp's voice was no longer steady. The Ambra sounded tense now, too.

Paul hit it and a set of icons appeared in the bottom center of the heads up display in a small circle. In the center was an icon of the ship with a few tiny dots swarming immediately around it. Further away, a set of three larger shapes dashed towards it from the edge of the circle.

She's right, that's two escort starfighters and a troop transport. She will soon be overrun, and they will destroy or disable us. You must launch. Zyp's voice had lost some of its mirth. The Ambra sounded almost grim.

A pit formed in Paul's stomach. This wasn't happening.

"Paul, you must go, I'll be fine," Edolit said, her voice strained.

He knew she was only saying that to get him to leave.

"I can't do this alone," he whispered.

"Yes, you can. I did it, too. Go. Make a difference." Her voice was calm and reassuring.

"I'll try my best."

"I know."

Left Panel, Small Lever. Slowly pull the lever towards you to engage lift, Zyp commanded, breaking off their forced goodbye.

Paul did, and the ship rose off the ground as he pulled the lever. He took the steering column in his shaking hands. The controls fit into them with a surprising familiarity. Each side had a grip similar to a gaming joystick and a series of switches and buttons, easily accessible by his thumbs.

Left Panel, Large Lever will engage thrusters. Enemy ships 15 clicks out and closing fast. It's now or never.

He pulled the lever and was pressed into his seat when the ship lurched forward. He pulled the controls towards him, angling the ship towards the sky. As he picked up speed, the weight on his chest made his breath come in shorter puffs, and his vision clouded.

The sound of Edolit's voice brought him back from the brink of unconsciousness. "Zyp, Command Override Code 114."

Command Override Code acknowledged, Voice authenticated - Commander Edolit Vyn. Training Mode Disengaged. Welcome to the team, Paul.

A stream of energy coursed through him and his mind cleared. He felt stronger, more in control.

"Good luck, Edolit," he said. He felt stupid, like he should say something more profound, but his mind blanked.

"You too, soldier," she said. He swore her voice was full of something that seemed pretty close to pride.

A burst of static in his ear made him wince.

A message flashed in his HUD: [Communications lost].

Paul lowered his head. It had to mean that they'd gotten her. He gritted his teeth and steered away from the incoming ships.

"I guess it's up to me now," he whispered.

And me, Zyp chimed in.

Chapter 9.

Prepare to engage cloak, Zyp ordered.

Paul's sweat made the switch slick against his fingers as he tried to steady his nerves. He kept his other hand tightly gripped on the controls, pointing the ship directly into the fluffy cloud ahead. Two starfighters were gaining on *the Specter*. With their greater speed, they were moments from firing range.

The viewport filled with wisps of gray as the ship plunged into the cloud.

Now, Zyp said.

Paul flipped the switch, and a faint shimmer flashed across the energy shields around the ship. Nothing seemed to have changed as they continued soaring through the murky gray. He looked down in confusion and gasped when he saw the combat map on the console was dark.

"What happened?!"

Cloak tech blocks all active scans from inside and out. They can't spot us with their instruments and we can't use ours.

"What about their eyes? Can't they see us?"

Nope. Look outside.

Paul stood and looked out the viewport at the sharp slant of the ship's snub nose. The ship's hull now looked like the clouds surrounding the ship. The image crackled and didn't perfectly blend with the clouds, but was realistic enough to give him the impression of the cockpit flying alone in a cloud without a ship beneath them. The projection was convincing enough to cause a wave of vertigo and make his stomach churn. He scrambled back to his seat, reeling.

The ship takes pictures of the environment around it and the cloak field projects it over the hull. A sharp eye could see imperfections, especially along the margins, but they'd have to be pretty close to see it.

Paul relaxed and sank into the pilot's chair. He veered the ship deeper into the cloud cover to be safe, but the tension faded from his shoulders; they'd escaped.

And Edolit hadn't.

Paul's shoulder slumped. Any relief he had disappeared, replaced by a wave of loss. He'd barely known Edolit, but he certainly would never forget her. He wished he knew more about her, how he could help honor her memory; he'd never even learned the name of her species or where she came from.

Edolit was a Hylian. She came from the third moon of Hylia. Zyp's voice was devoid of its usual mirth.

"Thank you, Zyp."

Paul watched the gray clouds spin around the ship, his mind swirling its own chaotic spiral. His body might not be tired yet, but he was mentally exhausted. So much had happened in the short time he had with Edolit. He couldn't process it all, and he wanted to let himself curl up into a tiny ball. But he couldn't rest yet. Edolit left him a mission to finish, and he would not let her down. Not the first being to believe in him in a long time.

"Should we head for space now?" His voice cracked and sounded weaker than he felt.

Go for it. They shouldn't be able to track our drive's heat signature and trajectory now that we're deep in the cloud cover.

For good measure, Paul changed course and waited a few seconds before angling the ship away from Earth. He held his breath, hoping the Varanul's starfighters wouldn't see them emerge from cover and shower them in laser blasts. Seconds later, he exhaled sharply as the ship broke through the cloud cover and headed towards the stars. Despite the atmosphere's dull haze, the stars looked brighter than he had seen in years.

It was only then that a wave of realization washed over Paul.

He was going into space.

A lifelong dream he had given up on long ago was about to happen. So much had changed in a day.

The air grew thin around the ship and the dusty wisps of the atmosphere faded away as the ship passed the threshold into space. Twinkling stars focused into unwavering pinpricks of light and multiplied. No longer filtered from view by the protective haze of the atmosphere, a beautiful tapestry stretched before him in the endless expanse.

It was breathtaking. Tears formed in his eyes as he looked out at the eternal expanse. He let go of the chair and waited to float away.

Uh, you've got to disengage the grav coils if you want to do that, bub.

"Oh. Right. Grav coils. I knew that." IIe wanted to ask where the switch was, but a flash of guilt made him hesitate. He'd have plenty of time to goof around later. Edolit had trusted him to complete her mission, and he owed it to her to see it through. Plus, those starfighters were still close by.

The Gate's location is programed into the navigational computer, it can calculate the best route. Hit this switch on the console.

A flashing arrow appeared in Paul's vision, pointing to a square button at the top of the console. Zyp's ability to anticipate his needs was another thing that would take Paul a lot of time to get used to. A detailed map of the solar system projected on the viewport HUD, complete with a haze of tiny dots to represent the asteroid belt and objects of the Oort cloud at the boundary of the system. The number of objects in the outer systems far exceeded any map he'd ever seen released by scientists on Earth. The solar system was way more crowded than they knew.

Tap this point on the screen. That's the Gate. Zyp projected another arrow towards a small object just beyond the orbital path of Saturn.

Paul tapped the object and a message box appeared: [PLOT COURSE? YES/NO].

He hit 'yes' and a series of dashed lines branched out in dozens of directions between their position and the hyper gate as the computer cycled through potential paths.

The ship will take a moment to calculate the course. Might be good for you to rotate the ship so you can see the planet before we go. It will give you practice on the controls, too.

"That's awfully thoughtful of you, thanks," Paul said, surprised the artificial construct in his head had thought to see his own planet from space before he did.

Just doing my job. Plus, it'll keep me from having to listen to you whine about not seeing it before you left.

Paul sighed. He'd enjoyed the moment of concern from Zyp, but it seemed to have passed already. He supposed their relationship had to start somewhere.

A tap of the screen minimized the course calculations to one corner of the viewport, and Paul gripped the controls and experimented with their responsiveness. The ship dipped and jerked side to side until he got the hang of it, and then he spun the ship on its axis. A heartbeat later, the view of his home world filled the viewport.

The ship was still over North America, the continent only visible by the twinkling lights of city sprawl dotting the shadowy landscape. To the east, the sun peeked around the horizon, illuminating the edge of his world in a large crescent. The brilliant blue of the Atlantic and the greens and browns of Western Europe and Africa slowly passed beneath them as their orbit brought them closer to the light side of the planet.

All the pictures he'd ever seen of Earth from space had never quite done it justice. Now that he was seeing it himself, he decided the majesty was impossible to capture in any image.

"Wow," he whispered, wishing some of his friends were there to see it.

The thought hit Paul in the gut when he realized he hadn't

said goodbye to anyone. He was leaving everything and everyone he had ever known, and no one would know where he was. All they would know was his apartment had been destroyed by a mysterious fire and he'd disappeared. Frantically, he scrambled for his phone and tapped the screen.

Your phone won't work.

Paul felt stupid. Of course it wouldn't work in space. He started to put it back in his pocket and paused. He took a quick picture of the spectacular view before he shoved the phone in his pocket. The photo might not capture the majesty, but it would be a good reminder of it. Surely an advanced alien civilization would have a way to charge his phone so he could see pictures of his planet. And his family.

Actually, we're in low enough orbit that you might pick up a satellite if it weren't for the cloak field. For the first time, you weren't being completely stupid.

Paul considered dropping the field to check for a signal, but he knew it wouldn't be worth the risk of discovery. Besides, who was he going to call? At this hour, almost no one he knew would be awake unless his father was drunk in some bar. While well in the realm of possibility, he wasn't going out of his way for that kind of goodbye.

I wonder how long it would take him to notice I'm missing? The thought left a bitter ache in his heart. Paul and his father had never really talked long before he'd even left home. Not since Paul's mother had died and his father stopped trying, anyway.

Rachel would probably be the one to notice he was missing, other than whoever was investigating the fire in his apartment. Even then, she'd only notice because he wouldn't show up to work tomorrow. His other friends, well, they'd probably find out in a couple of weeks after he didn't show up to one of their game nights or return a random call. Thinking about it now, regret gnawed at him, at all those years spent without close connections.

Then again, it would make leaving his world behind easier, wouldn't it? Maybe he'd come back one day and try to build better connections. First things first. He had to ensure there would be a world left to come back to.

The flash of an alert appeared on the viewport screen. The computer had plotted their course. Paul took one last glimpse at the swirling clouds of his home, trying to etch it into his memory. Before he could change his mind, he spun the ship on its axis and pulled the controls towards him. The stars streaked past as he vectored the ship back toward deep space. He was somber as he tapped the screen and brought the system map back to full size.

Tap anywhere on the course and confirm in the box to engage the autopilot. Unless you want to stay awake for days.

"How long will it take to get there?" Paul released his grip and set the autopilot. His stomach lurched as the ship corrected its vector on its own and engaged thrusters. The sensation faded after the ship's inertial compensators balanced the forces.

At little over five days, I estimate.

"Five days?! Isn't there a warp drive or something on this thing?"

Zyp filled his head with a sound that reminded him of a scoff. *Aren't you even a little impressed you'll travel over a billion kilometers in a few days when it would take your planet's technology months, if not years?*

"You're right." Paul sighed. "I'm just worried I won't make it in time."

You're doing fine. Go get some rest or explore the ship, there's nothing more you can do. Besides, I need to focus my processing power on finishing this damned assessment scan.

Paul had barely noticed the small icon in the corner of his vision move since Edolit had given the command for Zyp to release his training mode, and he hadn't really had time to ask about it.

"What exactly is this 'initial scan' thing you're doing?" he asked Zyp.

I'm analyzing your memories, knowledge, skill set, and basic physiology.

"Memories? Like everything that has ever happened to me?" He leaned back in the chair and tried to imagine what the Ambra would dig from his memory.

Yes, everything. Even that time Chris Jenkins flushed your head in the toilet. You really should have punched the jerk.

"Great. That seems a little invasive."

Well, I am in your head, after all. The more I learn about you, the better off we both are.

"I guess so. Then what?"

Then I can augment your abilities and make up for your weaknesses.

"What do you mean?"

Ugh, I was hoping you weren't as dense as these memories seem to indicate. I mean, you never noticed Rachel was trying to get you to ask her out, right? Are you blind? I can augment your physical and mental abilities. Like today, when I made you able to run longer than a block without nearly passing out.

"Okay, so you can give me super speed or something?"

Well, I might if we're bonded for a long time and you actually exercised once in a while. The longer we're bonded and the more experience we both have together, the more I can augment your abilities.

"Kind of like an RPG?"

Exactly like that. Only, well, I can't do magic. I wish I could. That sounds pretty sweet.

"Okay, so what about my weakness? What can you do about those?"

The first thing I'm doing after I finish this scan is uploading the control layout of this ship's cockpit so I can stop giving you directions like an eight year old. You know, it's a miracle your species doesn't eat their young with how dense you all are.

"You can teach me things directly? Load me up with everything I need to know, now!"

Sure I can, if you want to be a turnip. I don't know

what a turnip is, but it sounds terrible. Anyway, I can encode knowledge into your brain, but only smaller amounts at once. Too much can overload your neural pathways and cause some...problems.

"What problems?"

Well, death for one. Stroke, blindness, incontinence. Should I keep going?

"So, it's the same for everything else, too?"

Pretty much. Do the work on your own, I can make you better at it or help you remember. You'd already be encoding it in your brain after all, I'd only be reinforcing what's already happening. But take the easy way and directly download information too often, then you don't give your brain time to integrate the new pathways and... Zyp filled his head with the sound of an explosion.

"Got it. I'll go get familiar with the ship and leave you to it then." He stood up and yawned. "Or I'll get some rest."

Great. I'll engage your Heads Up Display so you won't have to ask me what everything is.

"Thanks." He started to turn from the viewport to explore his new home, but the moon captured his attention. Paul watched the moon passing above the ship. There was plenty of time to learn on the trip to the Gate, but for right now he wanted to allow himself a moment of awe.

He was in space.

He was in space, on a ship he was learning how to fly.

Paul smiled and flicked a switch on the console to turn off the gravity coils, and exhilaration prickled his skin as he floated into the empty air. Yes, the world was in danger, but he had to experience zero gravity for the first time. Afterwards, he'd explore the ship and go through some flight maneuvers to get a better feel for the controls.

At that moment, floating alone in the cabin of a spaceship was enough. He drifted until his head pressed against the clear viewport. As far as he could see, the vast expanse of stars stretched out before him.

It was more freeing than he'd imagined in his wildest

fantasies. He let himself savor it, if only for the moment.

Chapter 10.

Captain Ulec Numoh stood quietly on the bridge of the Gryx cruiser *Wildfire*, his thin arms clasped behind him, his uniform crisp and clean. His large black eyes reflected the glow of readouts scrolling across the tactical display hovering at his station, his face impassive. The flashing lights of the scrolling reports cast a dull glow over his pale gray skin. He was tall for a Gryx at just under two meters, and used it to his advantage, looming over his subordinates. Despite his age, he still received the respect demanded by his station. He didn't care if it came from his reputation or his stature, as long as it was there.

Around the bridge, techs and officers bustled at their stations, all Gryx except for pairs of Varanul stationed as guards beside his station and the bridge entrance. These sentinels were unnecessary in this backwater system, but Numoh prided himself on how tightly he ran his ship. He might command an operation in a backwater system, but he would treat it with the respect of a seasoned captain, if only to stay in practice for his inevitable return to civilization. When The Syndicate took their rightful place at the top, they would reward the Gryx with positions at all levels. His species had been The Syndicate's longest supporters, from when the grand plan had been whispered in the shadows of corporate boardrooms and smuggler cartels decades ago.

As Captain of a warship at its lowest alert level and a stable orbit, he had little work on the bridge, but he always showed up on time for his rotation. Long ago, results of his analysis concluded his crew ran 9.2% more efficient by his mere presence, and was reason enough for him to maintain his schedule. Like all Gryx, he prided himself on margins of efficiency. This was part of what led him to leave the Federation, along with most of his species. The plans of the Syndicate were far superior to the Federation, with its sprawling bureaucracy, blockages to free trade, and elevation of the weakest species among them. Numoh's face flickered with a sneer at the thought. The Federation was lunacy at its finest. The Federation had to fall, and Ulec Numoh was more than happy to help push it further over the edge.

The time of reckoning was nearly upon the Federation. Final targeting of key exploitable assets were already staged throughout the border regions, and the Syndicate had been infiltrating key positions of power for decades. Only a few more standard rotations and the time for attack would come. His lipless mouth slits curled into a smile at the thought. After all this time, the Syndicate would finally emerge from the shadows and claim its rightful place in the galaxy. The cracks in the grand pillars of the Federation would break, and under the Overseer's guidance the Syndicate will remove the waste from the galaxy.

And Captain Numoh could finally return to the core worlds as a hero of a new regime.

The bridge doors slid open and a tall Varanul walked purposely onto the bridge, directly towards Numoh's station. He recognized it instantly as Lieutenant Thrak, the troop commander for the battalion of Varanul stationed on the *Wildfire*. The Varanul was larger than most, and covered with deep gouges in his slate gray scales, including a deep scar running across his face. His scars and stature made Thrak an even more effective commander for the troops. The Varanul might be programmed to respect their creators, but the creatures truly worshipped those among them that had the tenacity to survive the battlefield.

He strode up to Numoh, saluted roughly, and gave a barely acceptable bow. Numoh ignored the near-insult. The Varanul were useful warriors, but he'd long since given up on teaching them proper decorum. He met the beast's center pair of eyes with just enough disdain to remind the Varanul who was in control.

"Lieutenant Thrak, do you have something to report?"

"Captain Numoh, we have the leader of the Resistance operatives in our custody," Lieutenant Thrak said in its harsh language.

"Excellent news, Lieutenant."

Emotions were hard to read on the faces of the Varanul, but Numoh caught a subtle shift in the Lieutenant's demeanor.

"There is more to add?" he asked.

"Yes sir. Unfortunately, the resistance commander proved harder to capture than expected. Our units were forced into open engagement before she went to ground."

Numoh stared at the Varanul. "Were there any witnesses?"

Thrak bowed in acknowledgement. Numoh saw a flicker of shame in the creature's red eyes.

"Sloppy, Thrak. Very sloppy." Numoh considered the implications. That settlement was among the smallest of their targets, a target of opportunity, really. A small mining operation interest only. The mess should be easy to contain, but if the primitives don't buy the coverup.... Well, he may have to accelerate the attack and add a new target to the list. He looked back to Thrak. "Were proper cleanup protocols followed?"

"Yes, sir. All bodies were recovered without further problem, and I informed the human ambassador of the incident immediately."

The ambassador would work hard to convince the populace the entire ordeal was an unauthorized recording event by an entertainment conglomerate. A fictitious spectacle, and not an invasion. The shell corporations would claim responsibility and the entire event would be swept away. It could have been worse. He studied the Varanul again. Something else was wrong.

"What else aren't you telling me?"

"We were unable to capture their ship. We used it to bait their commander as you instructed, but apparently the Resistance recruited a human. The human managed to launch the transport while the commander was engaging our forces."

"Why did you not destroy it, as Contingency Protocol 7.3 demanded?" Numoh had lost control of his speech pattern, despite himself.

The Varanul flinched at Numoh's sudden display of emotion. "The ship launched and cloaked under cloud cover before our starfighters could engage. They could not track the ship's trajectory."

Numoh stared at the Varanul, and fury overtook him. "Are you telling me the resistance ship is en route to whatever hole their fleet hides in at this very moment?"

"Yes, Captain."

"That is... most unfortunate." Numoh stared at the screen, thinking. The ends of his long fingers pressed together. This situation was quickly becoming chaotic. He had to regain control immediately, before it got worse.

"My apologies, Captain." The Varanul bowed its head, its taloned hands showing the proper gestures of subservience for the first time.

Numoh bristled at the sudden proper decorum. *So the Lieutenant was always capable of propriety and chose not to.* The thought only made the Captain more angry. He channeled that anger into a series of barked orders.

"Dispatch Alpha Squadron to search for the transport. Divide the squadron into four flight groups and search the probable routes to the Gate. Scan for drive signatures and residual heat. If they use thrusters to burn fast for the Gate, scanners will pick up something we can use to track them."

"Yes, Captain."

"Bring the captive to the *Wildfire's* interrogation room immediately. I must find out what they know."

"Anything else, Captain?"

"Launch all bombers of Beta Squadron. We are ahead of the Council's timetable, but the time to strike is now."

"But the council..."

Numoh raised a dismissive hand to interrupt the Lieutenant's objections.

"Has given me final authorization for the order at my discretion in an emergency. If this transport evades us, we must already control this system when their fleet arrives. Execute attack order Delta-7. You have my orders, Lieutenant."

The Varanul paused and cocked its head. Numoh never had read the reptilian creature's facial expressions perfectly, but he decided Lt. Thrak was hesitant to attack the planet without the full invasion fleet.

"It will be done, Captain." Lieutenant Thrak bowed his head and lurched toward his station to relay the orders.

Despite himself, Numoh allowed excitement to take hold as he looked at the tactical screen of the Terran System. Soon, he would watch the military bases of the pathetic primitives burn under their own creations. Ambassador McDowell would send the appropriate plea for aid to bypass the Federation's no contact protocols, and The Syndicate would have another system under their control. Numoh would be richer for it, but more importantly, he would be freed from the monotony of backwater worlds and take a step back towards the civilized glow of the core.

Numoh turned to Commander Keul, his second in command. "The bridge is yours. I will be in my quarters awaiting news from the Ambassador."

***

Captain Numoh watched the figures running across the screen and scowled, the lipless slits of his mouth pressed tightly together. The image of the resistance operative and a human running through crowded streets and the chaotic scene of bystanders filled the tactical display on his desk. His anger surged.

The Varanul had been extra sloppy in their pursuit this time.

Things had been going so well. Now, on the eve of the greatest coordinated effort his species had ever attempted, he had been given this mess to clean up.

He leaned back in his chair. The human ambassador wouldn't be pleased. The chime of an incoming transmission sounded, and Numoh groaned. He'd hoped that he would have more time to come up with an appropriate response before dealing with the human. He accepted the transmission and an elderly human face projected above the desk.

"Captain Numoh, what is the meaning of this?!"

Numoh met the holographic figure with all the calm the Gryx were famous for, not that the creature on his screen would recognize him for it. This human filled him with disdain more than others of their despicable species, which made it hard for Numoh to maintain his composure. Numoh hadn't decided if his reaction was because of the way the creature's flesh sagged off of its face in sickening jowls that resembled a lowly amphibious creature, or how this one had clung to power long after its mind and physical prowess should have allowed it to hold positions of power in any decent society. Most likely it was due to how easily it had been to convince the groveling weasel of a "leader" to sell out its own people for the promise of preferential treatment and wealth for its petty faction members. As useful as collaborators were, Captain Numoh held any being in contempt for being manipulated to aid in the subjugation of their own worlds so easily.

"Ah, Senator McDowell. I was expecting you." Numoh kept his voice cool. In the back of his mind he reminded himself how humans were easily manipulated, as long as he kept his emotions properly in check. They were a prideful bunch and lashed out when insulted.

"Do you realize the mess your operatives left in Franklin? I don't know if I'll be able to cover it up this time. A dozen different videos have surfaced online and we're having a hard time containing them. We might have a full blown crisis on our hands!" McDowell was flustered. His voice abnormally strained, his double chin flapped in the wind, horrendous and undignified.

"I am aware of the situation, and I apologize. Unfortunately, the incident could not be avoided." Numoh fought back the urge to hurl thinly veiled insults at the weak thing.

"Is there a problem I need to be aware of?"

"No, we apprehended the saboteurs before they could jeopardize the Franklin mining operation. The incident was unfortunate, but we had to pursue these operatives to protect our interests. However, we will need to push up our time table, just to be safe."

Numoh allowed himself the pleasure of a smile when he saw the color drain from the horrid creature's face.

"It is time? But... no, we are not ready," McDowell whispered.

You mean the hole you're going to hide in isn't full of fineries yet, you mean, Numoh thought with a glimmer of disgust sneaking past his diplomatic veneer.

"You're ready when I say you are ready. Don't forget who you're dealing with."

The human shifted uncomfortably.

"Of course. I will start the preparations," McDowell muttered.

"See that you do. And remember our accord, your people disarm and work our mines, and we let them survive. Any resistance and they will join the rest of the world in annihilation."

McDowell gulped and nodded. "Our leadership knows their role. We can keep our people in line."

"I sincerely hope so." Numoh paused and focused his gaze on the pathetic creature. "I do not enjoy eliminating potentially valuable resources and workers needlessly. But I will not hesitate to wipe out your species if I must. Keep the transition free of rebellion, fulfill your contract, and everyone profits. Are we clear?"

"I understand. Thank you, Captain; we are ready to serve The Syndicate. God Bless you."

"We are your gods now, Senator. You'll do well to remember that."

The creature bristled at the comment but kept its jowls still. Numoh held its gaze, relishing in the way the creature's skin grew ashen the longer it had to meet his eyes. The way its quiet defiance crumbled under his stare. He waited until it looked like the creature might crack before he released the creature with a dismissive hand wave.

"Go. Make your preparations. The attack plan will be tight beamed to your communicator within the rotation."

Numoh cut the communication.

Numoh was relieved to not have to look at the creature's face anymore when the hologram faded from his desk. He couldn't wait to get away from this backwater system. It had been a long time coming, and he was ready to seize his reward for leaving the Federation. The Council had promised him a post to a central planet if he completed his job in the Terran System without incident. He looked forward to being back in a real civilization again and not languishing away among primitives. He'd watched them for years, even walked among them with in disguise and sampled their "culture" that the Federation's council was so hell-bent on protecting.

Some planets he had watched over in his decades of service had made him question his loyalty. Peaceful beings with a sense of wonder and curiosity that had tugged at his heart when he had given the order to send them to the mines. Without the council's righteous goal, a desire to bring order, wealth, and stability to the peoples of the Federation, he might not have been able to give the order.

It helped that the council paid him well, especially for these backwater posts no one wanted.

Yes, McDowell will do his job, and I will be moved up to a more important role soon enough, he thought, allowing himself to enjoy the anticipation of victory.

Chapter 11.

A sharp, familiar *ding* rang in Paul's head, and he flinched. The bright chiming bell tone sounded like an oven timer going off. His HUD flashed with a message: [INITIAL SCAN COMPLETE].

"What was that?!" he asked.

I finished my scan! I liked that tone in your memory, so I thought I'd use it for notifications! Zyp was entirely too excited.

"Wonderful. What now?" Paul grumbled. He pushed off the bulkhead and drifted down to the deck with ease. The pull of gravity returned with the flick of a switch on the console.

His HUD flashed: [SET UP VOICE START COMMAND].

Speak whatever command you want used to start my voice interface.

"Zyp," Paul said, not feeling particularly creative.

Very original.

[START COMMAND SAVED. SET UP VOICE SLEEP COMMAND].

Now speak a voice shut-off command.

"Get Bent, Zyp."

Oh, nice. I like that.

[SLEEP COMMAND SAVED. VOICE COMMAND SET UP COMPLETE].

"I meant it as an insult."

I know, glad you have some spunk in you, kid. Now, from here on out you can speak or think commands and I will respond either way.

"Do you already know what I'm going to say?"

No, but I give a 97% probability you will mostly choose to speak commands out loud unless necessary because you think it will be less awkward.

Display status, Paul thought, crossing his arms. Zyp was right, and Paul was petulant enough about it to be stubborn.

Very good, I didn't even have to tell you how to do that. Must be all those games you've played.

Paul's HUD filled with various measurements of his body systems, health, stamina, injuries, and physiological systems. Beneath it was a daunting list of skills measurements. Some were familiar like 'stealth' and 'mechanics,' but others were indecipherable like 'astrogation.' All together they made his head spin, and he closed the status display with a tap of a button on his Ambra.

"So, how'd I do?"

Decidedly average all around, much to my astonishment. I expected you to get more dismal ratings but the algorithms seem to find you moderately capable in most aspects. Except for pilot and gunnery. You somehow got above average scores there. Did you really spend 458 Earth hours playing a combat simulator called 'Galactic Command'?

"Uh, that was a video game, but it sounds about right."

Actually, it wasn't too different from some of our training sims. Worse graphics of course and our AIs are far more advanced, so they aren't as predictable as your game AIs. But for the most part, the game prepared you for the basic mechanics of space combat.

A sudden swell of vindication tugged at him. *See, I told you dad*, he thought. Years of being belittled for his hobbies by a man who wasted his life on the drink or the job flashed through his head.

Your dad seemed like a real piece of work, Zyp chirped.

"Yeah, we never saw eye to eye on anything," Paul said. He had felt almost nothing toward his dad for a long time, but he was surprised to find he was sad thinking about the man now.

It's almost like leaving Earth completely makes you consider all those unresolved questions like, 'Does Rachel have feelings for me?' or 'Will my father ever respect me?' Oh well, guess you'll never know. Zyp was a little too happy to be rubbing that in.

Paul's mind raced. Would he really never return? Sure, he'd always wanted to move away but to another state, not a whole different solar system. *I can't worry about that right now, I have to complete Edolit's mission if the Earth I know is still going to be there.*

"Let's make it so I can fly this thing without help," he said, choking down his feelings.

Okay, sit down. This is going to be disorienting.

Paul sat in the pilot seat and a prickling sensation crawled up the back of his neck and into the base of his skull. His vision flashed with a bright white, and a dull headache formed behind his eyes.

"Ow!" he yelled.

Oh, it's not so bad, it's a small upgrade. The headache will pass in a moment.

Paul shook his head slowly and rubbed his temples. After a few seconds, his vision cleared, and the headache passed. He peered at the control panel and realized it was as familiar as his computer keyboard at home. Throttle, shields, weapons, cloak controls, and dozens of other subsystems. Lights that had been background lighting for him now told him exactly how much power was left in various ship systems.

He knew everything about how to control the ship now.

"Holy shit."

Pretty cool, huh?

"It's awesome. Now, give me everything I need to know about these Varanul, so I can know how to fight them," Paul said eagerly. His hand wrapped around the control stick and he sent the ship into a spin, trying to get used to how responsive the control was.

Nope, you'll fry your brain. The more we are bonded, the less time it takes for the brain to integrate the new data without overload.

"Right, I forgot. Death, stroke, or pissing myself. How long before I can get another upgrade?"

At current bonding level, approximately one Earth week.

"Well, looks like I'll have to learn the old-fashioned way. Can you display reference material for me to learn?"

Of course, I have access to the full quantum library of the Federation. Would you like to start with '5000 Rotations: A People's History of the Federation'? It's highly recommended. Some reviewers claim it to be a little heavy-handed on its criticisms of the Federation's expansion era, but it was basically a horde of invading forces then, so it seems like fair game for criticism to me.

"Sounds dry."

How about 'Galactic Politics for Dunces'? A hilarious Trygellian comedian wrote the series. Reviews indicate it to be entertaining, but well researched.

"Get bent, Zyp." Paul rubbed his face in frustration. He needed a break. He didn't have the attention span to read anything at the moment, even though he knew a greater understanding of the conflict was important.

The quiet of the ship was a little unnerving, but Paul enjoyed having a break from the prattle of Zyp's voice in his skull. He walked down the corridor and explored the ship, wincing when he saw the blackened holes in the walls from where the Varanul's stray blaster bolts had gouged the metal.

That could've been me. The thought sobered him more. He knew the Ambra could heal him, but he also knew it had limits. He was wearing a dead crew member's second-hand device, after all. Burned out holes in the wall reminded him he didn't want to test its limits, so he hurried past.

Just beyond was a small common room, lit with bright lighting that flickered on when he entered the room. Strange machines lined the countertop and a small table projected from the wall. He looked directly at the machinery and studied them. The HUD flashed a green script beside each as he passed. Food processor. Water dispenser. Medical supply. Microbar. Food warmer.

Past the galley, the corridor had five narrow doorways, two to each side and dead-ending at one at the end. He hit the panel button beside the nearest door and the door slid aside. Inside was a small room with barely enough room to stand inside. A messy bunk was mounted to the wall, and the room was otherwise empty, save for a few panels that looked like they slid out from the wall.

Crew quarters, he thought. A guilty flash of invasiveness made him shut the door. The room across the corridor was the same, only slightly more decorated with strange, angular objects mounted to the wall.

"Zyp, are these all crew quarters?"

Oh, you want to talk now? What if I don't want to?

Paul rolled his eyes. "Just answer the question, Zyp."

No, just these four. The one at the end is the cargo hold.

Paul skipped the other crew's quarters and opened the cargo hold. Inside was a larger room, lined with stacks of cases of various shapes and sizes. A ladder along the back wall led to a small platform with the gunnery chair, for the dorsal turret he assumed. He stared at it for a moment, wondering if he could have used it to save Edolit.

He shook the thought away. He couldn't let himself get bogged down by what-ifs.

One wall had a storage rack, stocked with a diverse array of vicious-looking blades and weapons. He walked beside the rack, studying the readouts for each one in his HUD. Bolt throwers, laser blasters, plasma rifles, tactical blades of all shapes and sizes, and a few small cylindrical or round grenades of various types. He was disappointed that he didn't find one of the blades with the glowing edges Edolit used.

The rest of the room was arranged haphazardly. Some pieces of equipment in the corner looked like exercise machines. Abandoned electronic components on a table surrounded by tools. Something that looked like a game table with abandoned drink containers beside stacks of oval-shaped metallic cards.

The wall opposite the weapon's rack had four space suits mounted in clear compartments. The suits were sleek and gray, but looked far flimsier than he expected. He shuddered, imagining a thin layer of material separating him from the emptiness of space. One suit was larger and broad, with an insectoid helmet and a segmented body shape, but the other three were humanoid, in differing sizes.

"I guess the crew was pretty diverse, huh?" He said, looking back toward the suits.

Congrats, genius. Yes, Edolit's squad was from different worlds.

"Do you have to be so... sarcastic?"

Actually, I do; that's how K'tal wanted me. It is how my core programming was set to make him laugh. Unlike you, you humorless ape.

The mention of K'tal's name hit Paul in the gut. K'tal was dead, and his Ambra was hurting. He struggled to imagine a machine could mourn, but he could hear the pain in its voice and the bitterness lingering in how it interacted with him. He had K'tal's friend uploaded into his head and he knew nothing about the alien.

"Which bunk was K'tal's?"

First bunk on the left outside the cargo bay.

Paul nodded grimly, opened the door, and stepped inside K'tal's small cabin. He didn't feel right about taking one of the other quarters, not yet. He didn't know what happened to any of them. He knew K'tal was dead, which made this bunk Paul's now, he supposed. Paul sat down on the bunk, sinking into the heavy foam bedding.

Above the bed was a poster of a scantily clad humanoid alien of some type. Busty and sultry, the alien had blue skin and extra appendages coming from the back of her head like a dozen small tails instead of hair. Paul blushed at the sight.

***K'tal sure loved his ladies**,* Zyp chirped.

"Don't you have something else to do? Get bent, Zyp." Paul felt awkward enough without some strange voice cracking jokes.

The room appeared empty until he noticed a small control panel at the head of the bed. He opened the panel, revealing a small storage compartment. Inside was a worn blaster with a small leather holster, with three thin, black rectangular objects scattered beside it. The HUD system automatically displayed information on it.

[KT-79 LIGHT BLASTER: Power Pack Fully Charged. Shots Remaining: 250]

Paul pulled the weapon out of its holster carefully. It was heavier than he assumed it would be, but fit nicely in his hand. He turned it over and saw that the other objects in the compartment were extra power packs. With a quick flick of his thumb, a pack ejected from its housing on the side of the weapon. He practiced reloading the power pack a few times and let his mind wander.

He hadn't held a gun since the last time he went to summer camp as a middle schooler. He'd been a decent enough shot, at least for a 12-year-old, but he couldn't imagine being great with a laser weapon. Still, it was nice to have options. He'd have to check out the weapon's rack and see if any of the others were more comfortable. There was no telling what he'd be up against before all of this was over.

Paul slipped the weapon back in the holster and closed the panel. The next panel had some clothing, including various human clothes of a few different styles and some sets of uniforms made from the strange fabric Edolit wore. He thought about asking Zyp about it, but he still didn't want to deal with the Ambra. He scrounged around in a few more panels, but found little that helped him learn about K'tal. The alien was a soldier and didn't seem to have many keepsakes except for a small screen that showed a picture of a landscape more fantastic than any of Paul's wildest fantasies about alien worlds.

The landscape was dotted with great towering spires of stone, with beautiful bands of purples and reds streaking through them. They looked like the stalagmites that dotted the caves he had explored as a child, but on a much grander scale, reaching up toward a sea-green sky. Nestled among them were small settlements swirling from the base of the spires with a keen geometric eye, entire cities designed to augment the landscape from above with swirling patterns. Curved rows of rounded buildings spaced by bright bands of natural colors, plant-life as vibrant as any color found on Earth.

Paul laid back on the bunk and it formed itself around his body shape, as comfortable as any feather bed he'd slept on. Averting his eyes from the sultry alien gaze above him, he looked at the picture of the landscape. He assumed it was a picture of some important place on K'tal's world, and he could sense the sadness the picture carried. Without asking Zyp, he assumed this world had been devastated. This scene no longer existed. K'tal fought because his world's resources now fueled the profits of a group that Paul didn't understand. A vast, dark organization that placed profit above the preservation of beauty like the scene Paul held in his hands. An organization that wanted to do the same to Earth.

Paul would do his best to stop it. To get Edolit's warning to her superiors so they could help. He'd finish her mission and honor K'tal's memory, and his sacrifice. Despite his weariness, the weight of his thoughts kept him awake with lingering waves of grief. Eventually, the soft hum of *the Specter's* reactor made Paul drift into sleep, exhaustion finally catching up to him.

Chapter 12.

Edolit regained consciousness in time to see the cell's deck rushing toward her face. She landed with a dull, painful thud against the deck and her vision blurred, threatening to fade to black again.

She growled and pulsed frustration, unable to move and face her captors. She could tell by their stench that they were Varanul. The door to her cell closed with a whirring of mechanics, and her mind began to clear. She forced herself up and took in her surroundings. She was obviously in a cell on the command ship of the enemy. Her hands bound in front of her with binders of a generic design. Security camera mount above the entrance, and privy in the corner. Otherwise, she was in an empty white room, without even a bunk to lie on.

Nian status report, please, she thought.

Nian's calm purr filled her mind. **Welcome back, Edolit. You have sustained heavy injury, but I have repaired the more critical wounds while you were unconscious.**

Display wounds, Nian.

Without comment, her Ambra scrolled a long list of wounds across Edolit's vision. It made her dizzy at first, but she eventually was able to focus on the scrolling text.

[Incomplete fractures to 3rd and 4th left ribs. Four superficial blaster burns to torso, cauterized. Three deep lacerations to right thigh. Approximately two score superficial scrapes, burns, and shrapnel lacerations to all extremities. Display further minor injuries?]

Negative.

Edolit repositioned herself against the wall and winced when it pressed against her aching back. The Varanul had nearly overwhelmed her healing abilities. A few more well-placed slashes with their talons or a direct blast to her head or major organ systems would have killed her. They wanted her alive. That meant interrogations would start soon.

How long to heal?

The ribs will take a two cycles to fully heal, but are stable for now. Blaster burns and shrapnel wounds healing at 5% per Terran Hour, stamina at 5% per hour as long as you stay put.

Nian emphasized the last point. The Ambra sounded more like Edolit's mother by the day.

Edolit pulsed frustration. There wasn't time to heal completely. She had to escape while they assumed she was weakened. She grew more irritated when she thought about her lost squad mate and failing in her mission. Her skin flushed a deep maroon, the darkest shade of anger. She had to escape and make them pay.

Nian, override stamina regeneration. Shift all energy to healing.

Nian wouldn't like that, but the Ambra obeyed. Edolit had no choice. She could only take so much more damage before going into a coma, and her body resources were already strained from lack of nourishment. The Ambra tried its best to maintain homeostasis in the body, using resources equally, but sometimes the situations Edolit found herself in necessitated less delicate approaches.

Did you track our location like I asked?

I estimate over 12,102 probable locations based on trajectory and the troop transport ship speed ranges.

Eliminate all locations over 100,000 kilometers away from a gravity well. They have to be using a planetary body to shield themselves from detection.

25 locations remain. Shall I display?

Eliminate all locations under direct observation by Earth-based satellites and observatories.

Three locations remain, all are moons of the Jovian Subsystem. Shall I display?

Excellent. Package results and transmit to Specter Team Private Band. If Paul or any other of the team are out there, they'll get the data back to base.

Transmitting. Location pings received from Ja'el and Omaro, vitals stable. Distance calculated at 12 and 10 meters.

The faint green pulse of relief washed over Edolit's skin. She may have lost K'tal on this mission, but she didn't lose everyone. Not yet, anyway.

No location ping received from K'tal, quantum data readout indicates elevated heart-rate far beyond normal and atmospheric conditions matching settings for The Specter.

Her heart jumped. Paul made it off world and was heading towards the hyper-gate. As much as she wondered at his location, she hoped he remained cloaked for the duration. Even in the vastness of space, the ship's drive would be easy to spot in an otherwise primitive star system, even cloaked. Surely Zyp would consider that and keep him safe. A wave of yellow grief washed over her skin as she realized Nian had said K'tal instead of Paul.

K'tal was dead. She'd lost another soldier. Pain burned deep in her chest, but she forced herself to swallow it down. She couldn't afford to get distracted by that now. Two more members of her team were still alive on the ship. Edolit knew she could get them out if she focused.

She had to get them out. She pulsed resolve.

Nian, archive all data, communication, and images from K'tal. Start a new file for Specter 3 and rename 'Paul.'

Acknowledged, performing quantum data upload.

She'd grieve K'tal later. Right now, she had to come up with a way out. Edolit took in her surroundings more critically. Somewhere there was a flaw she could use to get free, she only had to find it.

The door to the cell slid open. An abnormally tall Gryx stood in the doorway, studying her with his arms clasped behind his back, his officer's uniform prim and proper. It gave him the cool, confident demeanor that his species was so well known for. Like all Gryx, the officer had a steel gray skin tone, oversized black eyes, and a thin, lipless mouth. The thin wisps of hair along the sides of its oversized cranium showed him to be middle-aged.

Behind the tall, slender officer, two Varanul held stun rifles at the ready, glowering at her with their reptilian gaze.

Perform facial analysis on the Gryx, Nian. Display any information you find.

A few heartbeats later, the results scrolled across her HUD.

[Captain Ulec Numoh: Former Captain of the frigate *Stalwart* with Federation Star Fleet Command. Dishonorable Discharge in 5413 PF after The Hylian Massacre. Current affiliation: unknown. Display battles and accommodations?]

"You," Edolit growled, pulsing anger.

"I see your little gadget has introduced us already, so I'll skip the introduction," Captain Numoh said. His voice was dismissive and infuriatingly monotone. "I am at a disadvantage, my dear. I recognize your species. After all, how could I forget Hylia? However, I don't have a computer whispering your Federation records in my ear. Who are you?"

"Ka'ilk, you monster."

"Now, now. No need to be nasty, Commander Vyn. You're better than that, at least according to what your crews' loyalty leads me to believe." Numoh stepped closer, his lipless mouth curled into a wry grin.

Edolit pulsed rage. She wished she had the energy to snap his spindly neck, but she knew she was too weak. His guards would have her subdued before she could even stand in the state she was in. Numoh watched her with a vaguely curious expression.

"Ah, yes. I forgot how your kind display their emotions. The darker the red, the more intense the rage, am I right? Such an interesting adaptation. I'm sure it made your ancestors marvelous hunters, being able to communicate without sound." He shook his head and looked down upon Edolit with a patronizing look. "Such a shame, what happened to your world."

"How dare you speak of my world, butcher? You were there. You know what you did. How much were you paid to ignore our calls for aid?"

"I was well compensated." His voice was matter-of-fact, completely devoid of emotion. He gestured to the walls of her cell. "And I was given command of this grand vessel, not some ancient border-patrol frigate with a leaking reactor core. My new masters reward the worthy, they don't squander them."

"At what cost? How many died to line your pockets?"

"Yes, I let your world tear itself apart. And I genuinely regret that it came to that. Your species was so much more worthwhile than these disgusting Earthlings. Too bad your leaders failed to make the appropriate deals to protect you."

"Too bad yours cares more about profit than what is right," she growled.

"What is right? My dear, we will bring order and prosperity to this galaxy. What could be more right than that?"

"Whatever helps you sleep, monster."

Numoh frowned and shook his head. "You and your ilk will never understand. You thrive on disorder. Yet, somehow, you got organized enough to become a nuisance. And with these Ambra you wear, you have made yourselves into a surprising effective nuisance. How your group of terrorists developed such advanced technology is of great interest to my benefactors."

"And who might those be?"

Numoh laughed, a jeering, low-pitched rumble. "I will be conducting this interrogation, not you."

"You'll get nothing from me, butcher." She pulsed the tone of resolve. Numoh's eyes narrowed.

"We shall see." Numoh unclasped his arms and revealed her Honor Blade. He casually handed it to the taller Varanul, a gruesome creature covered with deep scars. He met the creature's eyes and nodded. "You may begin."

***

Edolit bit her lip hard enough to fill her mouth with the coppery flavor of her blood. She would not give the bastard the satisfaction of hearing her scream.

Captain Numoh watched eagerly as the Varanul sliced into her stomach with the glowing edge of her own Honor Blade. She met his gaze as coldly as she could manage. The sickening smell of her flesh cauterizing tickled her nose and made her nauseous, but she stood tall.

Numoh raised a hand and Edolit let out a faint growl as the creature stopped cutting. He took the blade from the creature and looked down at it, turning it over and inspecting the glowing micro-blades.

"This blade is impressive. Such an elegant adaptation of your planet's traditional Honor Blades. If your people had these they might have been able to resist us, don't you think?"

Edolit glared at the Captain, pulsing defiance.

Numoh only smiled and brought the blade up to her neck. The warmth of the blade crept through the layers of her skin.

"Commander Vyn, are you ready to tell me how much your little band knows?"

She growled and spit blood towards the Gryx. She'd hoped it would splash against his face, but it fell short, landing near hit boots.

He looked down and shook his head.

"Now, Edolit, that is unbecoming for a commander such as yourself," Numoh said cooly. "Your team had such good things to say about you."

Edolit growled, her skin ripples flashing the pulse of challenge. Among the Hylian he would be honor bound to a duel, though she knew it was lost on him.

"I found it interesting that they said nothing, no matter what we did to them. Nothing, except they'd rather die than betray their commander. Such... loyalty." He moved closer and clasped her chin with his rubbery hand. "I see nothing here that should inspire such devotion, especially for a Hylian. They're so much more easily controlled compared to your crews' species. You will tell me what I need to know."

A faint, bitter smell tickled at her nose, emanating from his skin. It was a bitter, acrid smell that reminded her of the ozone of blaster bolts. Her mind clouded, and her vision waived. She felt foggy, pliant. *Yes, I will tell him anything he wants to know...*

Biological Agent Detected - Antibodies deployed. Nian's steady voice jerked her back from the brink.

A flash of warmth spread through her system as Nian combated Numoh's pheromones. The pressure in her head receded and her mind cleared. Numoh watched her with a confident sneer. He didn't seem to know the extent that her Ambra protected her system. That gave her an advantage.

This is my only chance, she thought. She rolled her head back, feigning the mental haze had taken her over. She imagined herself three shots deep of Argothian Liquor at the Jarvus Tavern, and made sure her eyes drooped in a stupor before she rolled her head forward.

She'd seen this happen to others on her home world and never knew what was happening. Her people had never been united, but she'd always wondered how so many would have turned on their own kind. Now she had some idea. Numoh's rubbery skin on her cheek made her want to cringe, but she fought down a reaction and allowed him to pull her face up to meet his.

Nian, have my dermal glands mimic the pattern on Yaslik's that last day. Edolit silently ordered.

Done.

Out of the corner of her eyes, Edolit saw her skin fade to a sickly creamy color with streaks of the disconcerting flaxen yellow of sickness. Just like the agents she now knew were controlled by the Gryx had looked during the fall of her planet.

"That's better. If only your team could see you know, to watch you spill your precious secrets." Numoh ran his hand over her head, and she kept herself from cringing. His touch was sickening. "Now, where is your base?"

"The moon of Pat'il III," she murmured, forcing her voice to remain monotone. That entire system was devoid of sentient life, but had enough biosphere on some of its moons for a small colony to survive. It would be a believable location for a base.

Numoh nodded. "And who supplies you with such cutting edge technology as this device?"

So that's why I'm still alive.

A horrible thought passed through Edolit as she imagined augmented Varanul. The developer had assured them that the Ambra would self-destruct upon user death without a command code like hers, but she'd never really believed that. Sometime, one would eventually slip through their grasps and be captured by the enemy. Then the Resistance would lose their only edge against the Varanul in direct combat. The creatures were hard enough to kill without regenerative powers and strength augmentation.

"The Star Corporation," she lied. The corporation was rumored to be a supplier for the Varanul, and she wanted to gage his reaction to it.

Numoh's lipless smile faded into a sneer, and he pushed her head to the side in disgust. "That was sloppy, Commander Vyn. You must know we have operatives in all our rivals. We'd know if they had anything to do with developing anything this interesting."

Edolit surged forward against her restraints and whipped her head forward. Numoh smoothly dodged her attempt at a head-butt and stepped back. The alien stared at her with a dismissive glower.

"I had hoped to be more... civilized with our interaction." Numoh looked at her with an almost pained expression. "I hope you can tell me where your little band of insurgents got the advanced tech, for your team's sake. I'm afraid their loyalty to you may cost them dearly. I wonder who holds your loyalty more, your cause... or your team?

Edolit growled. "You don't want to find out."

Numoh laughed, a deep throaty rumble. "I do. I most certainly do." He waved a hand to the Varanul, and the thing stepped forward again, igniting the cutting edge of her blade. A dull hum filled the small cell. Numoh turned and walked out of the cell, leaving her with the Varanul.

Did you get that? Edolit thought.

Yes, I recorded Numoh's reaction time. Running analysis now, Nian said.

Good. Let me know when you have his threat analysis complete. The team is running out of time, she ordered silently. _And dull my pain receptors again. The cutting is about to restart._

Chapter 13.

Paul woke up with adrenaline already coursing through his system.

Wake Up! The ship is under attack! Zyp wailed.

The ship lurched from the force of impact. Paul shot up and sprinted to the cockpit, wondering how he had remembered to reactivate the Ambra before falling asleep.

You didn't. And you didn't even say goodnight, jerk. It's a safety feature. I'm on watch any time you are unconscious. Lucky for us.

"How'd they find us? I thought we were cloaked!" Paul shouted as he scrambled into the cockpit. He lurched to the side when the force of impact hitting the shields nearly knocked him to the deck.

Unknown. Probably scanning for drive signatures or residual heat. They'd know to check routes toward the Gate. Cloaking isn't perfect, especially under drive. It's best when lurking behind asteroids to spy on hard targets, not fleeing.

Paul flinched when the shields protecting the viewport flashed red. A laser blast's energy dispersing too close for comfort. The energy dissipated along the invisible energy barrier and left a glowing flicker in the shields.

He made it into the seat and glanced at the ship's readouts.

[FORWARD SHIELD: 86%, REAR SHIELD: 65%].

He activated the weapons system and looked out to the sea of stars. The bright blue plume of a ship's drive trail glowed in the distance as a small fighter ship curved back towards *the Specter* for another strafing run. His Ambra projected a treat display beside the starfighter in his HUD.

[*Lancet*-class light starfighter: Threat Level 2. Armament: dual laser cannons. Shields: 100%. Display complete technical data?].

With a jerk of the controls, he angled towards the enemy ship, trying to line up the crosshairs with the small fighter. For the briefest moment, he felt like he was back at home playing Galactic Command. The ship lurched as another blast hit the shields from behind, reminding him of the very real danger of dying in the vacuum of space.

[FORWARD SHIELD: 85%, REAR SHIELD: 61%].

He checked the combat map at the center of the viewport to see how many fighters he was up against. The map was blank. Panic surged through him.

"Are those fighters cloaked too?" he shouted, still trying to veer towards the starfighter ahead of the ship. It had nearly completed its loop.

Of course not. You can't cloak something that small. Cloak tech blocks your instruments as well as theirs, remember?

"Great, so I guess these target computers are useless," Paul muttered.

The crosshairs still line up, don't they? They just don't tell you when to fire like your lame video games.

"Oh! Well, at least there's that."

Laser fire streamed towards the viewport as the enemy starfighter opened fire. Paul instinctively pulled up on the controls and shot away from the stream of fire in a steep climb. Before the enemy could adjust, he reversed the motion and tried to line up a shot on the fighter before it reacted. He held down the trigger and sent a flood of red energy bursts streaming from *the Specter*, firing wildly into the space around the starfighter, hoping for a lucky shot. Even if he couldn't score a hit, maybe the ship would break off and give him a half a second to figure out what to do.

A few of his blasts splashed against the starfighter's shields and it broke off its attack, veering away sharply. He had a moment to see the profile view of the ship. It was a dagger-like design with three small engines on the tips of angled wings.

Zyp let out a whoop that reminded him vaguely of a side character from a movie he'd seen about jet pilots when he was a kid. Why he was thinking about horrible 80s movies during a space battle, he'd never know, but it felt strangely appropriate. ***Nice! You scored a hit. Guess you learned a few things from those video games after all.***

Another fighter darted past the viewport. *Dammit, that means there are at least three of them,* Paul thought. He jerked the controls and veered away from the new fighter.

He only had a heartbeat to decide what to do. He could cut drive and float. The cloak would buy him an edge, and his momentum could take him far from the battle. But they'd have some idea of his trajectory from his drive and eventually scramble enough ships to find him. He could try to run and find somewhere to lose them, but they were a long way from any planetoid. He doubted the larger transport ship could outrun small attack fighters, anyway. Which really left only one option.

He took a slow breath.

Before he could question his decision, he deactivated the cloaking device and braced himself for a harrowing experience.

The viewscreen burst to life and he spun the ship in a random vector to buy himself time to assess. The enemy fighters would scramble to get a firing solution on him now that he was de-cloaked, but he needed a plan of attack. There were three ships streaking towards him on the combat map, two quickly coming together into a loose formation to his left, the other coming about below.

At the edge of his sensor's reach, three more blips appeared.

Great, they've got reinforcements on the way, better get out of this quick.

I concur, Zyp said.

Was that worry in the Ambra's tone?

Yes, it was, Zyp answered Paul's thought.

He moved to intercept the two on the left before they formed up and was elated when the crosshairs flashed green. He squeezed the trigger and fired a stream of energy into the right fighter. It tried to swerve off, but the pilot was surprised by the sudden direct attack. Paul scored a series of direct hits on it, its shield value rapidly decreasing in his HUD until it hit zero.

One more blast sent the fighter careening away from the battle before it exploded into a cloud of dust.

Well, I'll be a flurb milker, you aren't completely useless. Zyp's tone seemed genuinely surprised.

Paul didn't have time to respond before the ship shook with impacts. Both remaining fighters had recovered from their disorientation and opened fire.

Paul spun the ship wildly and set thrusters to full. A starfighter burst past his field of view, filling his front shields with a dull glow as a couple of its blasts pummeled *the Specter*. He pulled back on the controls hard and tried to loop around behind the ship, glancing at his shields.

[FORWARD SHIELD: 75%, REAR SHIELD: 50%].

I can't keep letting them chip away at me, Paul thought.

The fighter banked left, keeping Paul from getting behind it. He tried his best to match the maneuver, but the fighter moved away, its greater speed and maneuverability a clear advantage against the transport. Paul lurched as his ship took another hit from behind.

Real space battles were a lot harder than he ever could have imagined.

He reset his shields, knowing he'd have to take a few more hits in the rear before this was done.

[FORWARD SHIELD: 15%, REAR SHIELD: 100%].

He stayed on his target and lined up a shot. He managed a hit on the small ship before it shot up and away from his vector wildly.

Damn, those things are maneuverable, he thought. He tried

to match the maneuver but *the Specter* couldn't make the same tight turns as the starfighters. The fighter quickly faded from his viewport, and he knew it would eventually get around behind him. Bolts of laser fire filled his viewport. The pilot behind him fired wildly, no longer concerned about hitting its wing mate anymore.

I can't out maneuver them. Time to try something else, he thought.

Especially not the way you're flying. Paul could hear a grim tone in Zyp's voice. The Ambra didn't seem to think he'd pull this off.

"Oh yeah? Watch this."

Paul broke off pursuit of the first fighter and barrel rolled, ignoring the rapidly decreasing value of his shields and focusing on his combat map. He straightened out the ship, gripped the throttle, and waited. The red icon of an enemy ship lined up behind him and the ship lurched with a series of direct hits. The second flight group of starfighters was nearly in firing range. It was now or never.

Here goes nothing. Paul pushed the throttle as far away from him as it could go, and his stomach lurched.

The ship slowed quickly from the sudden reverse thrust, and his pursuer shot past in a blur, narrowly missing a collision. Paul smoothly pulled the throttle and squeezed the trigger, accelerating behind the enemy fighter as he shot wildly. He filled the space around the tri-winged fighter with laser fire. The starfighter didn't recover from Paul's rapid deceleration in time, and he managed to line up a clear shot. His steady stream of laser fire made the enemy ship's shields glow. It tried to break away too late, and exploded with a blinding flash. Paul flew straight into the rapidly expanding cloud of super-heated metal and dust.

With a blur of movement over the controls, he changed vectors, cut throttle to zero, and engaged the cloaking device. He held his breath, expecting the ship to rattle from impacts. He hoped the debris from the destroyed starfighter would make it hard for the remaining ship to pick up his trajectory before he fell off their scanners. It was a gamble, but it was the best he could come up with. The transport wasn't maneuverable enough for a dog fight, especially with three more starfighters closing in.

A few heartbeats passed before he relaxed. The ploy had worked. He was safe. The ship streaked away from the battle, using the residual momentum of his last thruster burst. His skin itched, and he sensed the last starfighter scanning for him, probably joined already by reinforcements. He'd at least bought some time. He checked his shield status.

[FORWARD SHIELDS 19%, REAR SHIELDS 11%].

"That was close," he muttered. He equalized them to 15% each, not knowing which direction an attack might come from.

"Do these shields recharge?" he asked.

Of course they do. 0.5% per second, baseline. But since you cut thrust, they should charge faster. Shall I perform a more precise calculation?

"No, that's okay."

Okay, so shields recharge pretty slowly. They can't hold up to a concentrated attack. Good to know, Paul noted. After some consideration, he adjusted reactor power from weapons systems to shields. He wasn't using them, anyway. Better to refresh shields while he was hiding. He leaned back in the seat, noticing his shirt was soaked with sweat for the first time.

"Well, that gives me time to come up with a plan." He got out of the pilot seat and realized he was shaking. His adrenaline had worn off, and he was drained. A sudden rush of nausea coursed through him. He rushed down the corridor, trying and failing to make it to the privy in the main hold before he vomited. Instead, he spewed onto the bulkhead outside his bunk, his body reeling. Paul had survived his first battle. He wondered if it ever got easier to handle.

You get used to it after a while. Might be longer than most in your case. Humans are feeble creatures.

"Get Bent, Zyp."

Paul leaned against the wall of the corridor. He was shaking, shock and fear finally overcoming his senses. He was chilled and wrapped his arms around himself, whispering repeatedly,

"I can do this."

He didn't believe it, but eventually his hands stopped shaking.

The bright sound of an oven timer made him jump again, and a small icon appeared in his HUD. *What now? I've got to make Zyp change that notification sound.*

"Zyp, what's that?"

Got it together? Kind of? Good enough. Incoming message... Zyp paused, and Paul could hear the surprise in its voice when it continued. **From Commander Edolit Vyn.**

Chapter 14.

Edolit's voice filled his head.

"Paul, I'm glad to know you've made it so far. I have been taken captive and transferred to the base ship for the Varanul. I'm including coordinates in this data file. As soon as you are through the Gate, have Zyp send out an alert to fleet command for intervention and send all data. Tell them the Gryx appear to have a major role in the Varanul's mission. Warn all operatives in the border worlds, I believe an attack is imminent."

She paused, and he heard a groan. She was alive, but obviously in great pain.

"Get to the Gate and bring the fleet to the system. This ship appears to be mobilized for action. I'm not sure how much more time you have. Don't worry about me, I have a plan to escape and free my crew. The Gryx hold them captive here, and together we will do what we can to delay their invasion. Good luck to you Paul, until we meet again."

Transmission terminated.

"Where did transmission come from?"

Transmission originated near a moon of Jupiter. Likely the base ship she's been trying to find and destroy.

"We have to save her."

Whoa there, Kulth Ranger. You're one scrawny

*human who's only ever been in one fight, which you
lost miserably if you remember correctly. You
barely survived your first battle, and now you want
to storm a capital ship?*

"We don't have a choice, we can't leave her."

*Sure you can. She ordered you to jump out of the
system and bring the fleet. That's how you help her.*

"There are going to be patrols the entire way between here
and the Gate! Do you really think I can fight my way through
them all?"

*No, we plot a path using micro-thrusts and
slingshot around gravity wells to float you there. It
will take weeks, but you'll slip by their scans.*

"They'll kill her before then."

*Maybe, but she knew that when she gave the order.
You do realize that by barreling in against her will,
you could screw up her plans and make her have to
save you, right?*

"I'm not a soldier. I don't have to follow her orders."

*I guess not. It's not a big deal though, it's only your
world's funeral. Saving your friend obviously takes
precedence over 7.5 Billion members of your species.
Don't you have any friends among them, too? What
about Rachel? Or your dear old dad?*

That hit Paul in the gut, and he deflated. Zyp was right, but
he couldn't get over a nagging conviction that going after
Edolit was the honorable thing to do.

"Look, we're stuck right now, anyway. Let me try to think of
a plan first."

*Okay, I'll interface with the ship and start plotting
the safest course to the Gate.*

"First, display the most likely warship the Gryx would use in
this system."

Zyp let out a very human sounding sigh, and a ship
appeared ahead of him. The cruiser was sleek, with soft lines
and angular panels that gave it a utilitarian simplicity. It
wasn't flashy, but judging by the armored weapons
emplacements along its surface, it was formidable. The front

section of the ship was large and heavily armored, with weapons blisters nestled between curving ridges that came to a point like the blades of a hunter's arrow. The ship was obviously designed for frontal assault, with the heavily armored bow acting to shield the bulk of the ship's major systems and hanger bay.

[*Xyanthin-class* medium cruiser: Level 5 Capital Ship. Threat Level: 8]. Hovered beneath the image.

Display all details on typical crew, weapons, and starfighter complements, he thought.

Zyp didn't even give a snarky comment. The Ambra seemed to be sulking.

[*Xyanthin-class* medium cruiser. Length: 500 meters. Crew: 1500 enlisted, 300 troopers, standard complements. Heavy Plasma Cannons: 12. Point Defense Light Laser Turrets: 24. Missile Turrets: 6. Hanger: 12 light starfighters, 12 heavy bombers, 2 troop transports standard allotment.]

Paul groaned. After taking out two starfighters by sheer luck, that still left 22 more fighters in the system.

"Zyp, did sensor's detect any other ships in the system when we last de-cloaked?"

Yes. Would you like a map of their last known locations?

"Yes, display next to the cruiser."

You didn't say please, Zyp said.

"Didn't know I had to," Paul said.

You don't, but it is polite in most galactic cultures. Except the Gryx, they're renowned assholes.

"Please display the map, Zyp," Paul said with a sigh.

A top down map of the solar system appeared, and he studied it. The Gate was above the plane of the planetary bodies, just beyond Saturn's orbital path. He spotted the ten fighters spread between *the Specter's* location near Mars, and the path to the Gate. He'd expected that.

What he didn't expect were the twelve other ships in four tight cluster formations halfway between Jupiter and Earth.

"What are those ships, Zyp?"

Last scan indicates twelve ravager-class heavy bombers.

"Can you determine their projected course?"

Of course.

"Do it and display it on my HUD," Paul paused, and the silent sensation of annoyance tickled at the back of his head. He rolled his eyes. "Please, Zyp."

The map lit up with yellow lines connecting all twelve of the bombers to various points on Earth. Paul's heart sank.

"Zyp, we don't have time to rescue Edolit or reach the Gate. They're starting the invasion now."

***

Paul was up and running back to the cockpit before he realized what he was doing. He vaguely registered Zyp's voice, trying to get his attention and raising objections, but he didn't care. He didn't know what kind of ordinance those bombers had, but he knew it had to be terrible if that was all they were sending. He scrambled into the pilot seat and strapped himself in. This would be a bumpy ride, no matter what he did.

"Zyp, compare bomber locations with this new scan and give me a projection on bomber speed. We need to plot an intercept course."

Paul hit the switch to de-cloak, counted to three, and flicked it back on. He held his hand on the throttle, expecting laser blasts to hit the ship at any moment.

The solar system map updated. The ten starfighters were further out in the system now, and the lone survivor from the last battle had joined another flight group. The bombers had progressed towards Earth, but not by much.

Good, they're slow moving. I might get to them in time. He also knew that the fact that they were so slow meant their weaponry likely included massive bombs.

The map updated with an intercept route. He'd reach them with just a few minutes to spare before they were in firing range of Earth. It was going to be close. He keyed in the intercept coordinates into the autopilot and set throttle to full. Thrusters kicked on, and he sunk into his seat. The inertial pressure pressed hard on his chest until the stabilizers compensated and he could breathe again.

"Zyp, bring up a tactical readout on those bombers and let me know what I'm up against."

A world of pain if those other starfighters catch your thrust on scan.

"I'll just have to hope they're looking in the other direction, won't I?!" Paul snapped.

The tactical readout replaced the cruiser and map display. The bomber was less elegant than the fight he had already encountered, clunky but still in a similar three-winged arrangement. Attached to its side was a pod covered in an array of launch tubes, with a fourth drive wing attached to stabilize it.

[*Ravager-class* heavy bomber: Threat level 3. Shield Strength: level 2. Armor: level 4. Speed: level 1. Armament: dual HP-43 forward mounted lasers, 8 *tp-717* anti-fighter missiles, 6 *db-44* heavy fusion bombs].

"Zyp, what is the explosive power of those bombs?"

100 megatons, that's...

Paul's stomach clenched. "Twice the size of the largest nuclear bomb on Earth, I know."

Paul paled. Seventy-two of those savage weapons were heading towards Earth. Millions would die if even one of the bombers made it to Earth. More, if governments panicked and launched their own weapons at each other; the missiles had been gathering dust in silos for decades, but he was certain they could be launched without delay.

With a few clicks, he rerouted all the power from all non-essential systems, plus 75% of life support and environmental systems to the thrusters. The ship was flying with only a quarter crew, so the scrubbers didn't need to work at full. The ship would get cold, but he'd be too distracted to care.

He needed every extra second he could to stop them in time. He also needed something else.

"Zyp, how long until intercept at this speed?"

Approximately 31.2 minutes.

"I need you to project any simulations you have on file for these bombers, I need a better idea of what I'm facing."

Chapter 15.

Paul watched the simulation play again. This time he had slowed approach speed to get another round of missiles off before the bombers broke formation. Zyp had taken known data about *ravager*-class bombers and predicted actions based on various species to give Paul an idea of how they might react.

Two fighters exploded as he watched, and the rest scattered into loose flight groups. Zyp showed the time it would take for a new target lock and launch, then a third exploded. By then the remaining 9 fighters had spread from their bombing formation and scrambled into an intercept course. One more exploded from a fourth missile before the screen cut out, indicating the earliest possible return fire from the bombers.

Dammit, I'll still have to dogfight EIGHT of them. He rubbed his shoulders, trying to release some of the tension.

It was the best he'd come up while the ship raced to intercept the bombers, and it assumed no ship picked up his drive signature. His entire plan depended on having the element of surprise.

Congrats, you got one more before they killed you.

"You're not helping, Zyp," Paul growled.

Excuse me? Didn't I just come up with a complex simulation on the fly and give you a pretty HUD show?

"Okay. Point taken. Any ideas?" Paul said.

Nope. Your planet is doomed.

"Maybe. I can still take out a few more of those bombers before they get me, though. Each one I destroy is six cities saved. It might give the survivors a fighting chance."

Well, you've only got ten minutes to think of something. I suggest you spend some of that time having your last meal.

"I'm not hungry."

Yes, you are, your blood sugar is becoming critically low. You can't save anyone if you get the shakes in the middle of a battle, and I can't help without bio-available energy to burn, can I?

"Fine, you win." Paul couldn't help feeling like he was being scolded like a child, but he let it go. It might do him some good to get out of the cockpit, if only for a moment.

Paul stretched while he walked to the galley. He didn't quite understand how anything in there worked yet, so he just pressed the quick meal button. A small brown bar plopped out onto his hand, and he sniffed it. It smelled like the cheap bouillon cubes his mother used to make soup with.

"What's this?"

Everything a growing boy needs. Protein mounted in complex carbohydrates, mostly. Some sugar. Some vitamins. It's great.

Paul took a bite and gagged, his mouth flooded with the taste of sugary meat broth with the texture of a bar of moist chalk.

Good, huh? It was K'tal's favorite.

"You'd think an intergalactic civilization would come up with better food by now."

Well, you get used to it. At least, K'tal did. Besides, you chose the meal plan for his species, the Grr'alis. It's quite impressive that you're eating it at all.

Paul took another bite and chewed the bar slowly, telling himself it was no different from cheap off-brand jerky from a gas station. It was good to have something in his stomach, even if it the texture was gross. After a couple of bites, he found he didn't mind the flavor, actually. He walked back to the cockpit, the weird nutritional bar slowly disappearing as he focused on the simulation. It reminded him of countless hours of casually eating garbage while playing games.

Playing games. He looked at the bar, and a plan flashed into his mind.

"Zyp, what happens if the missiles don't have a lock?"

You don't hit your target.

"No. I mean, how does the missile itself work without a lock?"

They fly straight forever until they hit something and explode, or their explosives degrade. They only have enough accelerant for 60 seconds. Afterwards, they'll just drift along at a steady velocity.

That's it, that's my chance.

"Zyp, reload simulation. I want to try something out..."

***

Paul flashed the cloaking shield off, updating his sensor data once more. The last thing he wanted was to miss a last minute course correction and overshoot his targets entirely. His tension settled as he saw the scan results, the course was still on target. No sign of the starfighters scattered around the system changing course to intercept him, bombers still proceeding on their course. Time to engagement, two minutes.

Zyp, despite his incessant prattling, was an excellent copilot. The Ambra had plotted a course that lined up perfectly behind the flights of bombers with a few well-placed bursts of the thrusters. Now the ship gained rapidly behind their targets, under perfect stealth. No thrusters, just pure momentum pushing them closer to target range.

Paul mentally prepared his shots again. Flying under cloak without the use of the targeting computer, he'd have to line up his shots perfectly so his missiles weren't wasted. Meanwhile, he would remain hidden from the bomber's sensors longer. He hoped the trade off was worth it.

Ideally, he'd take out the first three bombers before the rest even registered they were under attack. He was confident he could destroy more before they scattered away from their clusters and made it hard to line up shots without his targeting computer. At that point, he'd have to shut his cloak field off.

Then he'd be fighting for his life.

No, not for his life, for the lives of everyone on Earth.

No pressure or anything, Zyp said.

"Right, no pressure."

The bombers' ion drives glowed brighter, and he could see the dark gray of their hulls now.

Just a few more seconds. Paul took a deep breath and tried to find calm, to steel himself for another battle.

He'd been resisting the urge to de-cloak and shoot missiles from maximum range, letting the computer do the aiming for him. Every simulation he'd run had told him that wasn't the way to go, it gave the bombers too much time to react. No, this was the only plan with half a chance.

He gripped the controls and adjusted the aim to the central fighter of the rear formation with micro-thrusts, guiding the crosshairs between the ship's ion drives. This was it. There was no going back. The icy calm he felt was disconcerting, and for a moment he wondered if Zyp had filled his system with anti-anxiety neurotransmitters.

No, his plan was good, and *the Specter* was a better starship than the bombers. He could feel it in his bones. He waited for two more deep breaths until the ship was growing large in the viewport and fired.

The bright glow of the missile streaked towards the central ship while he quickly lined up the drive of the second and third ships. With snapshots, he sent missiles towards them. He managed to fire the third missile a moment before the first missile impacted between the bomber's drives. The explosion consumed the small ship in a heartbeat, and its wing mates shuddered from the brief pulse of energy.

The ship's wing mates didn't have time to swerve from the explosion of their flight leader before missiles hit their ships. One exploded on impact, taking a direct hit on a drive. The other spun wildly away, its weapons array severed from the main body and the ship rapidly depressurizing, leaving a faint trail of debris and gases.

Paul wanted to celebrate, but he wasn't out of the woods yet.

He banked right and accelerated, lining up the next bomber. The formations were breaking, scrambling to react to the invisible threat of *the Specter*. He imagined the targeting computers of six fighters on his left searching for the heat signature of his active thrusters, but he forced himself to stick to the plan.

Paul lined up a fourth shot and reflexively shot a missile and started lining up another shot before he registered the fifth ship's motion. He was in a state of flow, his movements coming without thought, *the Specter* was an extension of his body. The fifth bomber broke right as its wing mate exploded and Paul's fifth missile launched. His missile missed wide, blasting out into the starry expanse.

Paul ignored the escaping bomber, knowing it would need time to come about before it was a threat. He took a deep breath and lined up the final bomber in the flight group. Laser fire erupted across the viewport, filling the area around Paul's ship. He gritted his teeth, ignoring the occasional shudder of a laser finding the edges of his shields, and tried to anticipate the movements of the bomber ahead of him. It bobbed and tried to change course to set up the other bombers for a clear shot.

Just like Paul thought it would. He smiled and released his missile, pausing long enough to watch the missile explode against the bomber's launch tubes. The ship was vapor before the fires ran out of oxygen to burn. A wave of relief spread through him. He'd beat all his projections by getting that fifth bomber. He spun the ship wildly to avoid the onslaught of laser fire and switched his weapons to lasers.

"Now comes the hard part," he murmured as he turned off the cloaking field. The combat display blinked on, showing him the swarm of seven bombers swirling around his ship. He chose one at random and veered toward it, bright green flashes of enemy laser blasts already filling his viewport.

Chapter 16.

Captain Numoh held the deadly edge of Commander Vyn's blade to the light and examined its fine serrations closely. He switched the blade on and watched its edge blur, the rapid movement of the serrations making the edge waver. A microsecond later, the serrations emitted their brilliant fuchsia glow, super-heated by an unseen energy source beneath them.

He wondered what metal alloy the blade's designers had used. Somehow, it could withstand the combined strain of rapid movement and super-heating without losing the ability to slice through ferroucarbon like it was a thin membrane. Such a material would have a wide array of applications when the researchers isolated and reverse engineered it. Numoh imagined he would receive great praise if it led to advances in hull plating and battle armor for their troops.

He shutdown the blade and turned it over in his hand. It was too large for his grip, obviously not designed for the thin elegance of Gryx hands. Still, it had a sleek beauty even he could admire. He'd watched as the forces under Gryx control used the blades to slaughter entire villages of their own people, even compelled his fair share of the creatures with his own pheromones. Despite his history with the culture, Numoh never imagined he'd see another Hylian Honor Blade, and in a way he supposed he never would. The blade he held was a more advanced replica, an homage to a culture lost.

The blades, and the Hylian fighting style that accompanied them, had been fearsome for primitives, but they'd never been able to stand up to modern armor. The Council had deemed them too primitive to adopt, and too dangerous to leave in local hands. After the culling and the consolidation of Syndicate control, all the Honor Blades had been melted to slag. This one appeared to be something different, a more advanced weapon modeled off the traditional blades of the Hylian people. Someone had made this blade for Commander Vyn as a deadly tribute to her people's traditional blades.

Someone with a creative zeal for complex technology was helping the Resistance. First with the super-advanced augmentation, and then the most effective ship cloaking technology he had ever come across. This new advanced tech was making this small cell of self-proclaimed protectors into more than just a minor nuisance. Now, this group was also being supplied personalized advanced weaponry.

If the Syndicate didn't find whoever was supplying these malcontents with advanced technology, things would spiral out of control when they made their move. Instead of a quick coup and restructuring, these resistance fighters would turn the natural consolidation of power under Gryx rule into a protracted civil war. The cost would be enormous, and if the tech he had seen was any indication, the Resistance would be far more destructive than their numbers should allow.

Who is designing these creations for you? What would it take to take these wonders for ourselves?

Numoh was confident Gryx engineers could reverse engineer the technology behind the blade, and inevitably the cloaking technology when they capture a craft or a cloaking unit was recovered from the debris of one. The tech he was most interested in, the Ambras, was the one that would make them unstoppable if they could unlock its secrets and produce them in mass levels. Indeed, if he could be the one to discover the source, he would ensure his place in the new regime.

The entire Syndicate's significant might had only captured a handful of operatives with these wondrous devices. So far, all attempts to learn their secrets had failed. Between the Ambra's programming and the tenacity of the wearers, all had been destroyed through various self-destruct mechanisms, safeguards, and triggers. Numoh remained convinced that the only way they would recover anything useful about these devices was through psychological means. Now that he had the esteemed Commander Vyn under his guard, he knew he could get at least one member of her team to break.

A sharp beep sounded from his terminal. He placed Edolit's blade on the rack behind his desk, along with the other artifacts of his collection, and accepted the transmission.

"Yes?"

"Captain, we need you on the bridge now!" The comms tech was beyond panicked. He made a mental note to find out the tech's operating number and make sure they received more training on proper handling of operational stress.

"What is the problem, ensign?"

"The bombers, sir. They are under attack!"

***

Numoh burst into the bridge, unconcerned with appearances for the first time in longer than he could remember. This was no time for concern with decorum. The loud echo of his voice through the room made every tech, guard, and officer in the room jerk in surprise. "Report!"

He joined Commander Keul at the tactical station and analyzed the situation. Keul looked up and pointed towards the projections of the situation unfolding near the Terran home world. Half of the bomber squadron had been destroyed and were swarming around what Numoh assumed to be the Resistance transport ship.

"The transport engaged the squadron from close range while cloaked. Three were down before they even knew they were under attack, another two were lost moments later," Commander Keul said. The elderly Gryx was grim normally, but carried an even darker glower now.

"Scramble Alpha Squadron to reinforce the bombers," Numoh ordered.

"Already done, but the closest flight group is just passing

the fourth planet of the system. They'll get there long after the battle is over."

Numoh muttered a curse under his breath. He'd almost had the human once already, but he'd misjudged the primitive's skill. Now, he'd wrongfully assumed the human's only option was to get to the Gate and request reinforcements from wherever the Resistance rabble were hidden. He should have assigned a flight group to guard the bomber wing instead of scanning for the transport.

Another bomber disappeared from the tactical display.

This can't be right, even a handful of bombers should be able to beat an untrained human in a direct engagement.... His thoughts trailed off as he peered at the chaos unfolding. A realization flashed in his mind - the Resistance had installed an Ambra on the human. There was no other explanation. The technology was far more powerful than he had predicted if it could make an ace pilot from one of those primitives.

"How close are the bombers to their launch window?"

"Uh, sir?" Commander Kuel seemed confused by his request.

"Now, Commander!"

Keul hastily read his sensor readouts and looked up. "Twenty five thousand clicks."

"Have the flight leader, Beta-3, and Beta-7 break from engagement and start their bombing run. All other bombers will keep the human busy until their payloads are launched."

"Sir, they outnumber them six to one. Surely they can handle one ship."

Numoh turned from the tactical screen and met the other Gryx's eyes. "No, they can't, they're already dead. This way, they can at least complete their mission. Give the order."

"Yes, sir." Keul saluted and relayed the orders to the comms officer.

Numoh turned to the lead engineer and navigational officers, standing at attention to his left. He gave an order he'd been waiting to give for two rotations, since the moment he was sent to this backwater system. "Fire up the main drive. Prepare *Wildfire* to leave orbit. Inform me when we are ready to disembark."

The navigational officer saluted. "Right away, sir. Course?"

"Earth. Set thrusters for maximum drive."

The officers scampered away to get their teams working, and Numoh smiled. *Even if my bombers don't launch enough warheads to start the nuclear war between the nations of Earth like we'd planned, the Wildfire will make them bow to us, regardless.*

Chapter 17.

Edolit couldn't wait any longer. The dull vibration of the ship's drive powering up was shaking her cell. The warship would soon be on the move.

Status report?

Nian displayed her vitals into Edolit's heads up display. [Health: 75%. Stamina: 25%.]

Cauterized blaster burns remain unhealed as ordered. Rib fractures set, but still unstable. Thumb reattachment complete and functioning at 85% baseline, Nian said.

That will have to do.

I recommend allowing your ribs to heal completely before acting. They limit your range of motion and leave you vulnerable to critical damage if impacted.

Noted, but we don't have a choice. The rest of the crew is out of time. They'll start killing them to get me to talk.

Then I suggest protecting your left side in battle.

I will. Reset stamina rejuvenation to default.

Now that her basic injuries were patched up, she needed as much energy as she could muster for the coming battle. The more she relied on Nian to augment her motion, the more exhaustion she faced. She was an excellent fighter on her own, but she knew she would need an extra boost to free her people, especially in her injured state.

Her plan was fairly simple, to overwhelm the guards dragging her to interrogation and free her compatriots before the general alert sounded. She glanced at the gory mess on the floor in the corner of her cell. Nian had found the blind spot in the security cameras almost immediately. The hard part for Edolit had been finding an angle to chew off her own thumb and slip her wrist out of the binders without arousing suspicion.

She looked down and moved the reattached digit. It still ached, radiating the rhythm of pain up her forearm. The thumb no longer moved at the correct angle, but it wasn't useless as she'd feared it might be. She had positioned it as best she could for reattachment, but was off. Nian had healed it, so she wouldn't bleed out. If she made it back to base, the surgeons would have to grow her a replacement for it to restore full function.

At that moment, she only cared about saving the remaining members of her team. She glanced down at the binders still attached to her other hand and adjusted them to make her appear bound. Anyone inspecting the security feed closely would see she was free, but she'd have to risk it. The element of surprise was her only chance.

She turned towards the door. Carefully, she hid the gore from the camera with her body and kneeled, her weight balanced on the balls of her feet and legs spread wide. Numoh knew enough about her people to recognize the meditation stance and, hopefully, would not suspect an attack. She closed her eyes and waited. Part of her hoped the Captain would be waiting behind the door when it opened. Edolit forced that part of herself aside with a cleansing breath. Revenge wasn't as important to her as her crew.

She breathed deep and time passed, the cell not quite silent. The baseline hum of the large battleship grew louder as the drive warmed up. Edolit brought calm to her mind and forced her muscles to relax, focused on her breathing and her mission.

The anxiety of waiting might have made some lose grit, but

she was a scout. She was used to lurking in the shadows and waiting for an opening to learn the enemy's secrets, striking only when an opportunity presented itself. Every moment she waited in her state of semi-meditation, the more stamina she would have in the coming conflict. The urge to check her status to see how much of her resource increased gnawed at her, but she resisted the temptation. This was her one shot at escape. She would have the energy she had and nothing more.

Nian interrupted her state of semi-consciousness. ***I detect three incoming guards, two Varanul and one Gryx.***

Engage combat speed enhancement, Edolit ordered.

Engaged.

Energy passed through her entire body. It felt like every muscle was vibrating with power. In a way, she supposed, they were. The Ambra's nanotech was flooding her muscles with energy and neurotransmitters, priming it for battle.

The door slid open, and she pounced without hesitation, driven by pure instinct. The door wasn't completely into its housing before she darted through the narrow opening and slammed into the shocked Gryx crewman with the full force or her weight. Her momentum sent him sprawling back, and he hit the floor with a loud crack, his head bouncing on the deck. The world blurred as she spun her leg and caught the knee of one of the Varanul in her sweep. The creature howled and hit the ground with a grunt. Her spin completed, Edolit slapped the weapon from the last guard's hand with a quick swipe of the binders still hooked to her right hand.

Still a blur of motion, she brought the binders down visciously across the creature's face in a backhand smack, catching two of its eyes by chance. She sprang into the air and caught the stunned Varanul's chin with her knee, narrowly avoiding the blast from the recovering guard behind her. The creature lost its balance and tumbled back, arms flailing. Edolit landed with a roll, narrowly avoiding franticly aimed blasts, and scooping up the guard's dropped blaster. She stopped her roll in a low crouch and fired two quick shots. The blaster fire stopped, and the Varanul slumped to the ground, two smoking holes bored into its chest. The remaining Varanul had recovered and roared defiantly, extending its talons as it lunged for her.

Edolit fell away from the creature's lunge and fired on instinct. Her shot burned through the Varanul's lower jaw before severing its spinal cord. It crashed to the ground next to her, limbs still twitching with nerve impulses.

Disengage combat speed enhancement, Edolit thought, her heart racing. She collapsed to the deck, breathing heavily, her chest struggling to rise against the pressure of the artificial gravity. The exchange had only lasted seconds, but she already felt drained. She'd gotten lucky. A third Varanul instead of the crewman, and she wouldn't have succeeded.

Disengaged. No alarms detected. Two enemy troops neutralized, one enemy crewman regaining consciousness.

Edolit scrambled to her feet and checked the corridor out of habit, arm shaking as she held the blaster outstretched in front of her. Though Nian would have detected another guard coming within earshot, her training still made her perform a sweep out of habit.

The crewman's dull groan made her spin around and level her weapon on him. He was a young Gryx, his rubbery gray skin covered in the remains of the gelatinous protein paste from her meal plate, unarmed. She hesitated. No need to kill this one. His glossy black eyes widened as he came to and saw the blaster leveled at him, and he jerked away from her.

"Where are my crew?" She asked.

"Please... don't...," he stammered.

"My crew," she growled, pressing the weapon against the Gryx's stomach and flashing the pattern of irritation. "An abdominal wound is a horrible way to die."

"Those two," the Gryx said, pointing to two cells down the corridor frantically. "Please."

Biometric scan data confirms this Gryx is telling the truth.

"Key disc," she growled, holding out her hand and keeping the weapon leveled on the Gryx. Beads of milky white sweat coursed down the crewman's smooth gray face. *Ka'ilk, he's just a kid. They are recruiting younger and younger these days.*

"Here, take it. Just let me go." He gave her a small metal disk with two indented sides with data ports.

"Thanks. Now get in the cell quickly and I'll let you live," she said, motioning to her empty cell with her blaster.

The Gryx didn't have to be asked again. It scampered into the cell with muttered gratitude. Edolit smiled, pulsed gratitude, and closed the cell doors. She held the key disc to the door panel until it flashed red, locked.

A quick check of the dead guards and she found the cuff release cylinder and freed her other hand. She scooped up the other guard's blaster and cursed when she didn't find anything else useful on their bodies. She'd hoped to recover her blade, but she'd take whatever edge she could get.

Edolit started towards the first cell, and a wave of dark spots flashed across her vision. She leaned an arm against the wall until the sensation passed, her skin pulsing a sickly ochre.

Status, she ordered. Her arms shook as she aimed her weapons down the corridor. She could barely hold their weight.

[Health: 76%. Stamina: 4%. Speed and strength severely limited].

Great. Keep me going as long as possible. Engage emergency stimulant protocol.

Confirmed. Set Stamina recharge to full, but you will need sustenance soon. Adrenal Stim Protocol engaged.

Edolit hated to use stims. They made her jittery, clouded her mind, and affected her accuracy with a blaster. But she could hardly avoid them now. She could barely stand and any moment reinforcements could burst around the corner. She embraced the warm surge of energy that coursed through her chest as the Ambra forced her glands to work overtime. Her head pounded before she made it to the first cell, but she no longer felt like she was going to collapse.

She keyed the door open and stepped into the small cell. Omaro jerked up in surprise, his narrow eyes dark between the chitin armor plates of his face. The maxillipeds around his mouth vibrated with excitement when he recognized her. His enormous form was shackled in a dozen places with substantial lines binding him to anchors in the wall, the shackles tight against the armor of his carapace.

Edolit grinned.

"Give them a hard time, didn't you, Omaro?" She started releasing bindings with the key disc.

Omaro laughed his strange high pitched chortle, so uncharacteristically high pitched for his huge, armored form. His species spoke in a chittering tonal language, but his Ambra projected a basic translation, layering over his speech in a discordant harmony. "Of course I did, Commander. Almost got out too, but they threatened to decapitate Ja'el in front of me if I didn't relax."

"I knew you'd give them hell. There, that'll do it." Edolit released the last binder, holding the massive creature's chest to the wall. He surged forward, stumbling slightly, as if his legs hadn't been used for ages.

"Thanks, Commander. I knew you'd come for us," Omaro said. He paused, cocking his head to the side, and asked, "Where's K'tal?"

Edolit shook her head and held out a blaster. "He didn't make it. Take point, I'm running on stims."

The Scyllarian's maxillipeds twitched and its jaws tightened. Omaro took the weapon and nodded grimly. "What's the plan?"

"First, free Ja'el. Next, we sabotage this ship," she said.

"And after that?"

"Hope we find the hanger before they discover we've escaped."

Chapter 18.

Paul broke left sharply, breaking off from yet another engagement to avoid a missile lock. Since the bombers had recovered from their initial surprise, he'd only been able to take a few shots at bombers here and there.

The swarm had obviously trained in protecting each other as a group. By the time he lined up a shot on one of the slow, well-armored bombers, at least one other had lined up shots on him too. They danced around him in chaotic waves, making short strafing runs to keep his attention while one of them looped further away and tried to launch missiles.

Missile lock warning. Break hard now, Zyp chirped loudly.

Paul rolled away from the ship he was pursuing and changed vectors sharply. He admitted he would have been toast by now if it wasn't for the Ambra's attention to the sensor displays. Paul kept his focus on flying while Zyp fed him information, reading gauges and data in his peripheral vision that his conscious mind filtered away.

A bomber flashed across his viewport and he turned, trying to follow. By instinct he squeezed the trigger and sent a brief burst of blasts towards it. Most streaked wide past the bomber, but two splashed against the ship's shields, casting a dull red glow over the ship's hull before it streaked out of view.

Paul gritted his teeth and changed vectors again, sending

the nose of his ship straight down, stars spinning in dizzying lines across his field of view. His stomach lurched until the ship's inertial compensators dampened the effect. His sharp loop brought the bomber with the glowing shields back into view. He squeezed the trigger and rocked the bomber with a steady torrent of laser fire. The shields sparked and glowed with dispersed energy, then collapsed with a brief burst of incandescence. Paul's lasers melted the armored hull beyond them into slag until the bomber exploded.

Nice shot, only six more to go! Missile lock, break!

Paul cursed and spun right. The glowing blue orb of Earth passed across his viewport, a little larger than his last pass.

The dogfight is taking us closer to Earth. I've got to end this.

He eyed the combat map and tried to make sense of the angry swarm of red dots swirling around his ship. Two had formed into a flight group and were moving away, trying to circle him. He rolled towards them in an intercept course and targeted the closest with a tap of his thumb. A mark appeared around the fighter in the heads up display as they crossed into view. He adjusted his vector to line up the crosshairs with the bomber. They flashed green, and he fired, covering the bomber's shields with a red haze as his lasers splashing against them. The fighter broke formation, but Paul matched its speed with a quick throttle adjustment and kept behind the ship, peppering it with blasts as it tried to break away.

Missile lock...

Before Zyp could complete the warning, Paul flicked the switch to engage *the Specter's* cloak and stayed with his target. The green glow of his crosshairs faded as the cloak engaged and cut off his sensors. He'd be flying without sensor data, but the bombers could only shoot by line of sight as well. He kept the bomber in his crosshairs as best he could, bobbing and weaving with it as its squad mate's lasers started filling the space around Paul's ship. They likely saw *the Specter* as a rippling wave behind Paul's stream of laser fire, but that was enough to target. Some blasts splashed against his shields, eating away at his protection.

He grinned as a blast rocked the bomber when he pierced the casing for the ship's drive. *The Specter* peeled away from the swarm of debris hurtling along the bomber's former path.

Two more bombers flashed in his viewport and he veered towards them. Keeping the cloak engaged, he lined up his shot by sight and fired. The bombers split away from each other, his shots missing both of them. He kept on the left bomber, matching its loop and bracing himself for the inevitable counter maneuver from its wing mate when it would attack him head-on. He rebalanced his shields with a flick of his thumb.

[Forward Shield: 75%, Rear Shield: 50%].

Earth flashed across his viewport again, spinning past as he sent streams of fire into the bomber's shields. He glimpsed the distinctive glow of three sets of ship drives against the blue green orb of Earth, and panic burst through him.

They're starting the bombing run while I'm engaged with these two!

I agree, these two appear to be stalling us.

Paul cursed and broke off towards the flight group, switched his weapons back to missiles and disengaged cloak. He targeted the nearest bomber of the breakaway group and lined up his shot, ignoring the shaking of the ship as his shields took fire from behind. He held his breath as he watched the crosshairs flash yellow.

"C'mon, c'mon," he whispered, sweat running down his brow. He reset his shields to full rear, buying himself as much time as he could.

The crosshairs flashed red, and he squeezed the trigger, sending a missile streaking out towards the bomber. He targeted another bomber as the first attempted to break away from the flight group and avoid the missile. It was too late. The missile exploded between its dual pods, sending them careening off in opposite directions, tumbling apart in a rapidly expanding cloud of metal parts.

Missile lock, break.

Paul cursed and switched on the cloaking field again. Changing vectors, he switched back to lasers and fired randomly. He swept back and forth across the path of the remaining two ships, hoping to score enough hits to make them break off. He landed hits on each, and the red haze of their shields glowed around them. A sickening feeling passed over Paul when he realized they weren't breaking off.

"Zyp, how far are we from the bomber's launch window?"

Two thousand clicks.

Great, just a few seconds at this speed.

Paul stopped worrying about avoiding his pursuers and concentrated fire on the lead bomber. *The Specter* shook with impacts as the bombers behind him took advantage of the stream of fire he provided for them to pinpoint their target. His shots against the small bomber didn't find as much success. The transport was a larger target, and even hidden by the cloaking field, the pursuing fighters hit their target more often than he could without the aid of his targeting computer.

"Screw it." He switched off cloak and lined up the lead bomber in his crosshairs, watching its shields begin to glow red. The bomber bobbed and spun, trying to launch bombs before being destroyed, but Paul kept it in his crosshairs. It broke away at the last moment, fire streaming from several holes in his hull as it spun wildly out of control.

Paul didn't linger to see if the ship was destroyed, he knew it was out of the fight. He switched to the final ship ahead and filled it with concentrated laser fire. The ship's shields glowed bright red and then the ship broke apart. A small pod shot from the rapidly depressurizing hull as the pilot bailed from the ship.

Paul whooped and switched to target the nearest fighter pursuing him. A quick mop up of the last two and his world would be saved.

Fusion bombs launch detected, showing on display*.* Zyp's voice cut through his elation.

Paul's confidence collapsed into a sickening knot in his stomach. He didn't need to check the map. To the transport's left, a glowing stream of missile drive trails streaked away from a bomber he had assumed was pursuing him.

He'd failed. A bomber had launched while the others

distracted him.

A sharp jerk of his ship broke his moment of paralysis.

"What was that?!"

Rear shields failed, minor damage reported to outer hull.

Paul cursed and pulled hard on the controls to break away from the attacker behind him, rebalancing his shields. As he turned, he watched the bomber release its payload one bomb at a time. Each one a death sentence for a city streaking away from its launch bay, its drive trail bright against the swirling expanse of stars.

*****

Paul's instinct took over as he completed his evasive loop and broke for the launching bomber. Anger coursed through him, made his vision hyper focused. A fourth bomb launch made his cheeks burn.

The transport spun wildly, and he fought the urge to vomit as the inertial compensators failed to counter the rapidly changing forces. Paul's vision blurred, the edges of his sight speckled in black dots as the force of gravity threatened his consciousness.

A fifth bomb spiraled from the bomber as Paul completed his turn.

"No," he growled. "No more."

He opened fire with his lasers before he had completed the turn, filling the space around the bomber in a cloud of red bolts. He lined up the bomber in his crosshairs with a smooth micro-adjustment and the stream of laser fire streaking from *the Specter* found its target. As the bomber rapidly filled the viewport, its shields failed. Paul clearly saw his blaster fire break through the bomber's viewport before he broke away, the pilot's body drifting free from the bomber as the transport whipped by. The bomber continued toward Earth in a lazy spin, its engines engaged but no longer under pilot control.

Bomber neutralized. Five fusion bombs away.

"Plot intercept route while I deal with this last bomber."

Plotting.

Paul's stomach lurched as he spun the transport, trying to

bring the last bomber into his crosshairs. The bomber expected his move and scored another hit on the transport's hull before it veered away. Red lights flashed on his screen, but he ignored them.

Paul pushed the throttle to full and sunk into his seat as the ship surged forward. The bomber was quickly in his sights as he completed his loop, caught in profile as its slower speed and maneuverability kept it from coming around as quickly as *the Specter*. Paul's lasers tore it apart before the pilot could react.

A wave of grim satisfaction sunk in as Paul veered back towards the glow of Earth. He'd survived. The bombers had been destroyed, but his job wasn't done yet.

Course plotted, showing on HUD.

Paul ignored the glowing map that sprung up in his vision and rerouted all power from his shields, life support, and cloaking tech into the engines and switched weapons over to missiles. The ship was already picking up speed when he glanced at the map and saw the five missiles streaking towards the planet. Most were still in a row, but the first two launched were already veering from the deadly pack, heading towards different targets.

His best chance was to take out as many as he could while they were still clustered together.

He targeted the nearest and watched it light up in the viewport. He lined up the crosshairs and frowned.

"Why aren't the missiles targeting?"

For small targets, you'll have to get closer for the sensors to lock on.

Of course, can't make this too easy, can we?

"Will I have time to get them all?" Paul asked. His heart jumped as the crosshairs flashed yellow, showing the missile had entered range. He licked his lips and kept his hand steady on the stick, willing the targeting computer to work faster.

You've got time. Missiles are still minutes from being out of range.

Paul relaxed a little.

BUT, You've only got four missiles left. Zyp's tone was grim.

Paul's heart sank as the crosshairs turned red with a missile lock. He squeezed the trigger reflexively, his mind still churning over the information. It streaked away and angled towards the fusion bomb.

"What about lasers? For the last one?" Paul asked, already angling the ship towards the next bomb in the formation and trying to get a target lock. His vision flashed white as the first missile impacted the bomb and exploded, blinding him temporarily and leaving bright spots dancing across his vision.

Probability of hitting a target that small with lasers at the projected range will be approximately 10561409 to 1 at your current skill level.

Translation: one city was going to die no matter what, unless he got lucky.

"Okay. We save who we can. Give me projected targets on the three other missiles while I take this one out," Paul said, while the crosshairs flashed yellow. He hoped this one wasn't targeting the smallest city on the list.

I'm on it. Fifteen seconds to compute.

"Great, let me know when I have to decide who lives and who dies," Paul said grimly, squeezing the trigger as soon as the crosshairs pulsed red.

Hey Paul, you did well. Zyp's voice was a tone Paul hadn't heard before. Was that sadness?

Not good enough, Paul thought as he shifted the ship towards the next missile. Earth was large in his viewport now, swirling clouds peppering familiar outlines of the continents.

Chapter 19.

Edolit cringed when she saw Ja'el's arm laying on the table next to the small Grr'alis, lying in a dried patch of green blood, swollen and black with rot. Ja'el smiled weakly at her as she rushed to the pilot's side.

"They got nothing from me, Commander," Ja'el said. She coughed and spat blood onto the table beside her. "They really tried, though."

"I can see that," Edolit said. She nodded to Omaro to watch the door and handing him her blaster. The hulking alien blocked the door with his armored form as he stepped back out into the corridor.

Nian show me Ja'el's status.

[Specter Two - Ja'el: Health: 15%. Stamina: 5%. Critical injury sustained.]

Can we save the arm?

Negative. Her arm is past saving. Her Ambra stopped her from exsanguination, but since it wasn't reattached before...

Got it.

Edolit quickly undid Ja'el's bindings and helped the Grr'alis to her feet. She wavered slightly but could stand with some support.

"Sorry I didn't get here sooner," Edolit said, placing her arm around the pilot's tiny waist and helping her towards the door.

Like K'tal, the only other Grr'alis she knew, Ja'el had always been smaller than her, but Edolit was concerned with how much more emaciated she felt. Her muscles felt like they'd been eaten away, and Edolit could see her pink skin was pale and loose, hanging from the pronounced bones of her sharply angled cheek ridges.

"Nothing you could've done. They cut it off days ago. Kept threatening me with cutting off the one with my Ambra if I didn't tell them who made it." Ja'el stopped and looked at her with a haunted expression in her small gray eyes. "Guess they were hoping I'd cave if they let me watch my arm rot."

"Come on, let's get you out of here," Edolit said.

Red lights started flashing in the corridor. Omaro yelled in the doorway, "Time to go, someone finally checked the cell security feeds."

"Ok, change of plan. We've got to evacuate Ja'el. We need to get to the hanger and commandeer a ship to get off this heap," Edolit growled.

"Won't they see that coming?," Omaro said

"Yeah, but I've..."

Ja'el interrupted, her voice cracking and husky from dehydration. "The hanger should be empty. They've launched their bombers towards Earth and their starfighters are searching for our transport."

Edolit paused and looked at Ja'el, pulsing curiosity. "How do you know that?"

"Numoh likes to gloat too much. I think he thought it would help break my spirit. Or maybe he just enjoyed listening to himself talk."

A wave of concern coursed through Edolit. *Nian, give me status and location for Paul.*

Paul last de-cloaked approximately 25.4 clicks from Earth and appears to be heading towards the planet. Health and stamina at 100%, but biometrics show him to be in acute distress.

Contact Zyp for status update.

Query sent.

Blaster fire rang out from the doorway as Omaro opened fire

with both blasters. He jumped back into the doorway, dodging return fire.

"Time to go, Commander! We don't want to get boxed in!" He fired once more, as if to add an exclamation to his point. The blaster bolts stopped flooding the corridor, and Edolit assumed his blast found its mark.

"Okay, take point. Ja'el, stay behind him and I'll take up the rear."

"Where to?"

"Still to the hanger, they'll have a shuttle of some sort at least. Take the long way to throw them off. Head towards the engineering deck," Edolit said as they reached the end of the corridor. She scooped up the blaster from the fallen crewman Omaro had shot, letting the Scyllarian keep both other weapons they'd recovered. "Let's see if we can cause some chaos to keep them guessing."

Omaro nodded and turned right, his weapons at the ready. She didn't need to tell him to have his Ambra plan the route for him. He was way ahead of her. She liked that about every member of her team, they were all adept at acting out implied orders and taking the initiative. For scouts like them, it was the difference between life and death.

Response to query received.

Report.

Zyp reports two enemy engagements. First was defensive engagement en route to the Gate. Paul disengaged after destroying two starfighters and went on the float, full dark. Second engagement is an assault on the bomber wing.

Edolit's skin flushed the bright violet of surprise. Did he really make a frontal assault on an entire squadron? *Result of second engagement?*

Bomber wing destroyed, minor hull damage to The Specter. Zyp reports Paul is currently attempting to neutralize fusion bombs launched toward Earth.

Edolit turned the corner behind Ja'el, surprised at the lack of resistance that they faced as much as Paul's performance.

Display battle statistics for Paul.

Nian displayed his stats into her HUD without comment. Edolit blasted a crewman who had the bad luck of opening his quarters to investigate the alert in front of her.

[Engagement 1: 3 *lancet-class* light starfighters. Enemies destroyed: 2. Damage Reported: 0. Shields lost: 85%. Lasers fired: 567. Accuracy: 11%. Missiles fired: 0. Missile hits: n/a].

[Engagement 2: 12 *ravager-class* heavy bombers. Enemies destroyed: 12. Damage Reported: 3% Hull Integrity Loss. Shields lost: 100%. Lasers fire: 2301. Accuracy: 15%. Missiles Fired: 8. Missile hits: 7. Fusion Bombs Destroyed: 2].

Edolit was impressed. Paul was performing far better than any other pilot she'd seen on their first mission. He'd ignored her orders to flee and taken out the bomber wing like she would have wanted. He'd also known to disengage when he was outclassed by the starfighters. She'd sensed that he was special when he had agreed to help her, but she was surprised at how well he was doing.

Did Zyp indicate why his performance is so proficient?

Zyp reports Paul has spent 458 Earth hours in a flight simulator prior to their bonding, his pilot aptitude far exceeds Zyp's expectations for his species.

Blaster fire made her duck back behind a corner, pulling Ja'el back and shielding the Grr'alis with her body. They'd been found.

Give Paul the coordinates to this ship and send him an order for extraction when he's done with the bombs. And give me locations for the enemies around the corner.

Done.

Edolit rolled out from behind Omaro and downed one of the Varanul with a quick series of shots from her blaster, using her Ambra's data to guide her aim. If she weren't on stims, she would have only needed a single shot, and she cursed her inaccuracy with a snarl. Omaro caught the other Varanul squarely in the chest as Edolit's motion drew its fire, and it dropped to the deck in a heap.

"Okay, let's get moving. Looks like we've got another ace pilot in the crew now. We just have to hold out long enough for pickup."

Ja'el and Omaro looked at each other questioningly, but said nothing. They trusted their commander completely and would get an explanation when the time allowed for it. She hoped they didn't see how tired she was.

Chapter 20.

The first choice had been an easy one for Paul. Saul Paulo was one of the biggest cities in the world. Paul felt a surge of relief when his missile tore the fusion bomb into a cloud of base elements.

Two bombs left. I project the targets to be Mexico City and El Paso.

Paul glanced at the combat map and groaned. The bombs were wide apart now as they angled towards their targets. Choosing one would vector him far away from the other. By the time he got a missile lock and fired, he wouldn't have much of a chance to shoot down the other with his lasers. He knew it was a long shot, but he would try, anyway.

Of course it would have to be two places I know. Paul thought about Mexico City, a sprawling city with bustling crowds of people. El Paso... well, it had to be another large city with a military base. It also happened to be where his father had moved after Paul's mother died, wanting to be closer to his old army buddies.

Paul blinked sweat from his eyes and decided, spinning the ship around his target and scanning for a lock. He didn't have time to second guess himself; the decision had been made.

Now he had to live with it.

Tears burned at his eyes, blurring his vision. He suspected Zyp was blocking his nervous system in some ways because he felt unnaturally calm, his hands steady as he waited for the crosshairs to flash from yellow to green. He blinked, tears breaking free from the corner of his eyes.

The crosshairs pulsed green, and he squeezed the trigger. The missile's drive plume was immediately lost against the backdrop of the bright planet below.

Paul didn't wait to see if the missile hit its mark. He had to have faith that it did its job. He looped back towards the other bomb and keyed for a target lock, his heart racing. Earth filled his viewport now, the bright blue of the oceans hiding the glow of the remaining bomb. He was completely reliant on his instruments and his augmented vision to find the plume against the brilliant colors of his home.

A small icon appeared on the HUD, and he angled towards it. The bomb was moving faster than before, pulled by Earth's gravity. His crosshairs flashed green, and he squeezed off a shot. The shot missed, the slight movement of the controls from the pressure of his finger on the trigger enough to make him miss such a small object.

You have new orders from Commander Vyn, you must break away.

"Quiet, Zyp," Paul spat. "We're not done yet."

Paul gave up on finesse, on trying to line up a perfect shot. His only chance was to get lucky. Hundreds of thousands of people's lives depended on him, his father somewhere among them.

Paul squeezed the trigger and held it. The steady stream of laser fire filled the space ahead. He kept firing, trying to line up the shot with micro-adjustments of the controls. He held his breath and willed a shot to hit its mark, for the bomb to explode. For the man he thought he had let go of long ago to be safe. For there to be some chance at reconciliation.

Hundreds of shots and still the bomb streaked towards the North American continent. Paul could see the glow of satellites now, streaking past in tight orbit around the planet, glinting as they reflected the sun. Close enough for the targeting computer to pick them up, his combat map filled with hundreds of targets flagged as unknown. He didn't let it distract him, even as the HUD display flashed red warnings around multiple satellites in his flight path. He kept firing, kept trying to make the crosshairs flash green.

Kept trying to save them.

The bomb glowed orange as it hit the atmosphere. Paul let himself hope it would break apart, that the rushed bomber was supposed to fire inside the atmosphere. He kept firing, willing the bomb's plating to melt away in the atmosphere. Or break apart in a burst of slag from a lucky shot. Or a secret space defense laser that was rumored to have been made in the eighties.

Paul was panicking, his hand shaking. His palms coated in sweat and vision blurred with tears.

Pull up Paul, the heat shields are rerouted to engines! The atmosphere will tear us apart!

Paul growled a curse and kept firing until the power ran out to the laser batteries. He watched the last shots streak from the ship and miss the bomb, leaving him staring at their fading glow. He kept squeezing the trigger as tears streamed down his face, willing one last shot to come. To make the shot. To save El Paso. To save the man who'd shown him the stars before his wife's death had made him become broken and lost.

Instead, Paul pulled on the controls and guided the ship away from the atmosphere, settling into a stable orbit. He rolled the ship, filling the viewport with the familiar outline of North America. He kept his eyes glued to the bomb until it faded from view and disappeared from the targeting computer's range. Then he watched the glowing lights of El Paso in quiet resignation until a bright flash of hellfire consumed it. Hundreds of thousands dead in a moment, without warning.

Somewhere among them, his last family member was gone.

Red messages flashed across the HUD, but he ignored them, focusing on the bright glow of the explosion fading into glowing embers as anything not vaporized by the explosion burned in the night.

Paul, starfighters have been on an intercept course since we engaged the bombers. The first group will

arrive in minutes. You must cloak.

Paul wiped tears from his eyes and tried to force himself to reset the power settings. His breath was vapor, the residual heat of the cabin long lost to the void of space. He stopped and stared at the embers, unable to move. He'd failed. He wasn't able to save them. He wasn't able to save *him*.

Paul. We must go.

Paul barely heard Zyp's voice. Something in him had broken. He had descended within himself, and the details of the outside world faded away. Visions of the explosion looped through his mind, and he imagined the heat of it searing his skin away. He was shaking, his body chilled while his mind overloaded with the imagined heat of a fusion blast.

Paul vaguely registered the flash of a message on his HUD while he imagined himself burning.

[Shock response detected. *Emergency override protocol* engaged].

Paul's mind continued to be lost in the fire, but he felt his body moving. He experienced nothing but a cool numbness, didn't want to do anything but sit and wait for the starfighters to tear the ship apart. He wanted to join the people he failed in a fiery blast. To join his family in quiet nothingness. Despite his nihilistic impulse, his body moved. With a detached fascination, he watched his hands moving over the control panel. He couldn't feel them anymore. They looked and felt alien, wrong. Like they belonged to someone or something else.

I'll take care of you, Paul.

His hands smoothly reset environmental control to 25%, set cloak recharge to full, and rerouted all weapons systems into shields. The motions were methodical and robotic under Zyp's steady control. He watched his hands move from a distant place, his mind locked out of his body, like watching a video feed.

While the cloak batteries recharged, Paul's hands punched in a series of coordinates into the navigational computer he didn't understand, strings of numbers separated by dots and commas. His mind fixated on the numbers, and his fractured mind interpreted them as the death toll, climbing exponentially.

Course set. Cloak recharge at 15%, Cloak re-engaging.

Zyp's words didn't break through Paul's haze. He stared at the navigational numbers, telling himself they were the count of the dead. Somewhere in his mind he registered the slight pull of inertia against the pit of his stomach, but still he stared. The view of Earth shifted in the viewport as the transport rotated and streaked away. Another message flashed in his HUD.

[*Emergency Override Protocol* Complete. *Twilight* Protocol engaged].

Paul's last thought before sleep was forced upon him was of the people he had just failed. Of his father, unspoken to for years, burning alone in the night.

Chapter 21.

The bridge of the *Wildfire* was silent as Captain Numoh forced himself to remain passive, staring blankly at the tactical screen. To the crew, he projected the calm indifference that his station as a leader demanded.

Inside, he was raging, reeling from the reports of a single target destroyed and the loss of his entire bomber squadron.

Years of careful planning and manipulation. Years of being trapped at the edges of civilization. All wasted. All because of one primitive human, barely of age in its own culture and ignorant of its proper place in the galaxy, had been seduced by rabble. The human had proved far more capable than predicted, ruining years of planning in moments. Even if a single bomber had destroyed their targets, the human governments would scramble to destroy each other with misguided counterattacks, helped along by the efforts of the human ambassador.

Instead, a single, minor target had been destroyed. A relatively insignificant military base in a mid-level city. News reports showed human governments already blaming terrorists for the blast. There would be no plea for aid by the Ambassador. No legal justification for Numoh to take control of Earth's recovery under the laws of the Federation.

It left Numoh with little choice. He had to order the orbital bombardment of the planet to begin as soon as the *Wildfire* was in range.

Commander Keul interrupted him. "Captain, we have been unable to locate the escaped prisoners. Shall I expand the search?"

Captain Numoh turned to his second in command and struggled to remain stoic. The disruption of the bombers was unfortunate, and his superiors would surely have much to say to him about it, but the escape of the prisoners was another matter entirely. No amount of explanation would free him of the stain on his station. Numoh could feel his position fading away. He'd be lucky to be Captain of an ore hauler by the time he regained order of the operation. The Resistance had foiled his every move, and if he didn't get the situation under control quickly and quietly, he stood to lose everything.

"Expand your search, and post guards at all nodes for critical systems." Numoh forced his turmoil to boil beneath the surface of his voice. The result was something that approximated the icy commands of an Admiral, and judging by the way his commander shifted uncomfortably, he was sure he hid his turmoil appropriately.

"Sir, we don't have the troops..."

Numoh's scowl silenced the aging Gryx. "Awaken all off-duty crew. Place all non-critical stations on minimum staff levels, and arm all remaining unassigned crew. Have them formed up into fire teams and search the ship. I want them recaptured or neutralized within the hour."

"Yes, sir. Anything else?"

"Keep me updated on the search for the Resistance transport. I don't expect the scum to show themselves again, but keep our starfighters on the search, anyway. That will be all for now, Commander."

Commander Keul bowed stiffly and turned to relay the order. Numoh watched the Gryx move slowly across the bridge with a cool confidence. For the first time in his career, Numoh wondered if he should be in control of a warship, if he should leave it to those below him who seem to move at ease in command. Turning back to the screen, he shook the thought away. Madness, he knew his place, and he'd show the petty world he was tasked with sedating soon enough.

Chapter 22.

"When's our ride get here, Commander?" Omaro chittered while he downed another Varanul with his blaster. He tossed the body of the crewman he had been using as a shield aside and turned to Edolit, his maxillae twitching questioningly.

"Unknown. Zyp reported in an hour ago before engaging cloak they had to go dark. Paul was in shock after the bomb impacted."

Ja'el stopped looking towards the corner for more guards, her remaining arm outstretched with her stolen blaster, and looked at Edolit in shock. "Paul? You recruited a human, didn't you?!"

Edolit nodded. "I didn't have a choice."

"General Thriss will not like that. You went against his explicit orders," Omaro said. He pulled the body of a Varanul away from the computer terminal and tossed it to the deck unceremoniously. It landed with a sickening thud.

"I think the General will forgive me when he sees Paul's performance," Edolit said. She moved to the terminal and began tapping the screen, the smell of ozone and burned Varanul making her wheeze.

"Well, I hope his resolve is tougher than his puny human maxillae if you want to make the case to the General."

Edolit opened the menu for the environmental controls and took the temperature control offline. Varanul were cold-blooded, and losing residual heat would slow them down.

"He'll make it. He just saw an entire city die. Zyp will make sure the ship is moving to pick up up while it sends Paul to sleep to recover from the initial shock," Edolit said as she continued her work. She knew the shock would likely turn into post-traumatic stress and Paul would feel the effects for years, but she kept the knowledge to herself. Edolit believed in him enough to know he'd pull it together enough to make the pick up.

She opened another menu and checked the crew assignment files.

Nian, copy files and analyze for crew numbers and deployment locations.

Copying.

Edolit opened each file quickly, allowing Nian a fraction of a second to copy the data from the screen, and then did the same for the troop assignment files and ship schematics.

A blaster bolt flashed against the wall to her left, and she flinched. Ja'el and Omaro pinned down the Varanul and laid down suppression fire to send its squad mates diving for cover.

"Time to move," Ja'el said.

Edolit opened one last file randomly and glanced at it for Nian. It could be a shipping manifest for sundries for all she knew, but she hoped it was something important. She stepped back and shot the terminal twice with her blaster. *That should cover my tracks,* she thought. She spun in time to send a blaster bolt into the forehead of a Varanul that had looked out from a packing crate it had been using for cover.

She tried to shift her aim to another Varanul that was firing towards Omaro, but her vision blurred and her shot went wide. Omaro cried out as a blast burned into his chitin carapace. She fired again, and the shot met its mark. The room quieted after the creature's death jerk sent one last blast splashing against the wall beside her. Her skin burned from the molten metal as the blast splashed against her arm, but she ignored it. She rushed to Omaro and checked his wound.

"I'm fine, Commander. Just a scratch," he said with a pained expression. "Doesn't feel too good though."

Edolit looked at the hole burned into Omaro's shoulder. The flesh beneath his shell was badly burned and oozing clear viscous fluid, but as far as she could tell his Ambra was already patching up the wound. The sight of the wound made her dizzy again, and her vision grew spotty.

"Good, can't lose another one of my team, today," Edolit said through a wheeze. She was having trouble catching her breath, with every movement of her chest sending shooting pain from her bruised ribs. *Damn, my stims aren't enough to keep me going at this rate.*

"I won't let you down, Commander," he said and then nodded towards the hall leading to the engineering deck. "Are we still moving towards engineering to cause some damage?"

Ja'el grabbed Edolit by the shoulder and kept her from swaying. "You okay Commander?"

Edolit nodded a thanks to the Grr'alis. "They'll think we're heading there now that we've taken out a few of their patrols. Now, we head to the medical bay. I'm running on fumes and we could use a moment to patch ourselves up."

Nian, give me the route least likely to have patrols based on the assignments we downloaded.

Done. Nian's smooth voice calmed her as a small map appeared in the corner of her field of vision. Edolit glanced at the map and then nodded back towards where the Varanul lay. "This way, we're not far."

They quickly searched the bodies of the Varanul as they passed. Edolit and Omaro now carried two small blasters each and a couple of spare power packs. As they moved on, Edolit noticed Ja'el frowning down at the third blaster they left lying in the corridor as they passed, and glanced down at where her arm should have been with a grimace.

Edolit came up to her side. "Hey, I'll make sure you get the best replacement in the fleet when we get home."

Ja'el forced a smile and met Edolit's eyes. "I'll never fly again, though."

"You don't know that."

"But I do. That was my dominant arm." Ja'el's shoulders

sunk. "They'll ground me."

"Hey. They'll try, but I won't let them. I need you on my team." Edolit was serious. Ja'el and Edolit had been through a lot together in the years of fighting a proxy war against the Varanul. She trusted the Grr'alis deeply and valued her, not only for her flying ability, but her unwavering courage. What Edolit saw now in her friend's eyes troubled her. She had come close to breaking, Edolit saw it in the haunted look in Ja'el's eyes. Edolit knew her friend would never be the same.

***

Nian guided them through the ship in a meandering path past darkened crew quarters, dodging patrols. They remained undetected, save for one unwitting crewman who had the misfortune of choosing the wrong moment to leave his quarters for the privy. A quick strike of Omaro's chitinous arm knocked the Gryx out cold. Edolit dragged him into his quarters and locked him in while he wet himself.

The med bay was empty, bright light filling the small room and left it devoid of shadow. Three exam tables sat empty, the diagnostic scanners in standby mode alongside them, primed for an influx of patients. The ship's surgeons were likely en route to the site of a skirmish to help the wounded Edolit's team had left behind intentionally. Anything to strain resources and increase confusion would help them.

"Patch yourselves up, we have little time," Edolit said, moving to take guard.

"You first, Commander. I'm good. I'll take first watch." Omaro shoved past her before she could protest. The hulking soldier took position near the doorway and kept both barrels of his blasters leveled towards the ends of the corridor.

Ja'el set her blaster down on a counter and started opening storage panels along one bulkhead. Edolit joined her, searching the panels on across the room. She pulled each panel down to reveal the supply cabinets and instruments inside, each panel folding down into a small shelf. She found the nutrishakes and chugged one down greedily. Edolit had escaped more wounds than the rest of her team, but the combat enhancements had wiped out her caloric reserves. She barely tasted the thick, chalky liquid, but felt the difference almost immediately when it hit her stomach.

Disengage stim protocol.

Are you sure? You are still only operating at 8.6% stamina.

Disengage stim protocol.

Confirmed.

Almost immediately, Edolit's mind cleared but at the cost of making her body feel like she was on a high gravity planet wearing full tactical armor. She was wiped out, but needed a moment to let her mind clear up from the effects of the stims before they moved on.

She finished the nutrishake with a chug and opened a second one, sipping it more slowly.

"Hey Omaro, heads up," she said, smoothly tossing a nutrishake to the guard before he could look. He holstered a blaster and caught the shake without taking his eyes off the corridor and bit the cap off with his mandibles.

"Thanks, Commander." The Scyllarian sounded disappointed. His species had a harder time than most consuming liquid foods, but he got most of it into his mouth slit.

She grabbed another shake and walked to Ja'el. The small Grr'alis was injecting herself with a pain suppressor, unceremoniously jamming the applicator into the meat of her leg and pressing the release valve. Edolit raised an eyebrow and pulsed the color of concern when she saw the other two applicators already lying empty at Ja'el's feet, but she left it alone. Her Ambra would block it from overwhelming her system.

"Here, you need some fuel too," Edolit said, holding the shake out to Ja'el.

"I'm fine," Ja'el said, her voice dreamy.

Great. Edolit sighed and held the shake in front of Ja'el's hand. "That an order, solder."

Ja'el let the applicator drop to the ground and snatched the shake away. "Fine. I'll take over watch."

"Ja'el..."

"I'm fine, Commander."

Edolit glanced at the spent pain suppressors and pulsed irritation. *No, you're not.*

Omaro appeared beside her and shook her from her worry.

"Find any gelpak's yet?"

Edolit's eyes flashed to the wound on Omaro's shoulder and nodded. "Yeah, I saw some over here. Let's get you patched up."

Together, they walked back to where Edolit had been searching and pulled out a stack of gelpaks.

The gelpaks were unnecessary due to the healing power of their Ambras, but they were always a plus on any combat mission. The more energy the Ambras expended healing them and producing hormones to keep them fighting, the faster their reserves would run out. The Ambras only augmented their existing systems, and only could do so for short periods of time. Eventually, their bodies would run out of material to metabolize and would shut down.

Edolit placed a pack on Omaro's shoulder wound and glanced back at Ja'el. The alien was keeping guard, but her head drooped. She motioned Omaro to look at her, and his face hardened.

"Keep an eye on her for me, okay?" Edolit whispered.

"Already on it, Commander. She had a rough time of it."

"Thanks," Edolit said as she finished stretching the gelatinous material over the soft flesh of his shoulder wound.

She eventually convinced Ja'el to place a gelpak over the raw skin where her body was still repairing the damage from her missing arm, as well as a few spots with burns and slices, remnants of the torture she had endured. Edolit wrapped another pack around the aching thumb she had hastily reattached, and another over her still bruised ribs.

The couple of minutes it took them to down as many nutrishakes as they could stand and patch up their wounds was worth the detour, Edolit decided when she queried her team status readout on her Ambra. All of them had recovered some stamina and health from the break. Not much, especially in Ja'el's case, but she hoped it would be enough. Paul's status was still a mystery, but she assumed he was still under the cloak. Zyp would make sure he got to the pickup.

"Okay, break's over. Time to move." Edolit's entire body ached, and she felt like she could barely move, but she resisted reengaging the stims to conserve her resources as long as possible.

Chapter 23.

Paul jerked awake, his arms thrashing wildly. Adrenaline surged through him as he nearly fell from the pilot's seat. The nightmare had propelled him from sleep and sent him back into the world swinging.

Calm down Paul. You are safe. Breathe.

It was just a dream, Paul told himself. Then reality set in. The amorphous being holding him down might have been a dream, but the memory of watching El Paso disappear was very real.

And the last of his family was gone in an instant. Family he hadn't spoken to in years, but family regardless.

Would you like a sedative?

"No! And don't put me to sleep again," Paul growled. No, he deserved every bit of the pain he was feeling. He'd embrace it. It had been his decision, now he had to carry it. "Where are we?"

A map flashed in front of Paul's vision, and he flinched. He was still waking up, and it took him a minute to make sense of it. The transport was en route to Mars, and the map showed Zyp had set the course to use the Martian gravity well to slingshot towards a large icon moving away from Jupiter. The command ship. Three sets of red icons showed the last known position of the enemy fighters clustered between Jupiter and Earth. Paul glanced at the console and saw that they were moving under zero thrust, cloaked.

"They're scanning for us, aren't they?"

Yep. Like a swarm of angry yellow jackets. Those stinging things sound terrible. They don't even make any delicious regurgitated ooze for you.

"How did you avoid the starfighters?" Paul ignored Zyp's attempt at humor.

Zyp let out an exaggerated, electronic sigh before answering.

I only used micro-thrusters until we were sufficiently blocked by Earth's moon from their scanners, then I burned hard for Mars.

"And there, we'll do the same trick to loop back towards their base ship and pick up speed."

That's the plan.

Paul nodded. With the starfighters scanning the space around Earth for his thrusters, the chances of their scanners catching *the Specter* were minimal. Zyp had come up with a good plan. Paul still felt a flash of anger course through him when he remembered the sensation of being unable to control his own body. He knew that he'd frozen, that shock had taken him over and Zyp had saved him, but he hadn't let go of the violation it entailed.

"Good job. Now don't take over my motor function without my permission again," Paul grumbled. He knew he was being petulant, but he didn't care. He had to lash out at something.

I can't promise that.

"Why not? It's my body!"

It's against my core programming. I can only allow you to self-destruct to avoid capture, and then only as a last resort.

Paul deflated. He hadn't really wanted to kill himself. Not really. The loss was just too much for him to take in. Sleep had done him some good, but the anguish ached deep in his core. He'd let down so many, but one he had let down long ago. He looked away from the viewscreen, his stomach churning. He wondered if he would make it to the privy before he vomited this time.

7,534,234,901.

"What's that?"

That's how many people you saved.

"And how many did I fail?," Paul said after a moment of hesitation, the course navigation numbers scrolling across the console screen haunting him.

681,728.

Paul nodded. He knew he'd never forget that number, but it wasn't as large as he'd imagined during his breakdown. The number would grow as the fallout affected the surrounding area, but he wouldn't be around to find that out. He would exact revenge for those people lost. He'd be fighting whoever was controlling the Varanul as long as he could. His grief was, at least for the moment, becoming replaced by deep, simmering anger.

"Hey Zyp," he said.

Yes?

"Thank you."

Just doing my job.

Paul managed a laugh at that.

"Well, how long until we make our burn?"

28 minutes.

Paul got up and stretched. His neck ached from sleeping in the pilot's chair and he rolled his head to loosen the muscles. He felt a flood of relief after his neck let out a loud pop.

"I'm going to get some food and then you can help me go over how to get Edolit."

Enter 21-870 on the meal processor. It'll be much better than the Hardokan meat bar you ate last time.

"Thanks, that was pretty terrible."

***

The food wasn't just better, it was perfect. He didn't know what the small greasy coils of food were, but they had a satisfying crunch to them and were filled with a gooey cheese-like sauce and protein. They reminded him of the poppers served at the bar near campus he used to order all the time.

Zyp had chosen something that resembled comfort food for

him without asking. Warmth stirred in his chest at the consideration the strange being in his head displayed. It was nice to know it wasn't just programmed for snarky asides and dad-jokes.

The thought hit him in the gut. His dad had never been much of a joker. Hell, he'd barely been a talker, but the thought of his father still hurt. Paul swallowed it down. He couldn't fall apart now. Couldn't go back into the dark place, not while there were still people who needed him.

Hunger sated, Paul sipped a cup of a sweet, moss-colored tea that Zyp had assured him was caffeinated and stretched his legs. He imagined the transport would be cramped with a full crew, but it was a lonely place for a crew of one. He considered trying some of the exercise equipment in the cargo hold, but couldn't quite make himself go through with it. Despite feeling better, part of him was dazed by the events of the past few days, like they weren't real yet. Shock, he supposed. Another part of him was too nihilistic to consider anything resembling self-improvement. That part of him wanted to curl up in K'tal's bunk - he still wasn't ready to call it *his* bunk - and sleep for a week.

It's almost time for the slingshot.

Paul slurped down the last of his tea and tossed his cup in the refresher. The tea had tasted like sweetened boot leather, but it had done its job. He felt more awake by the time he settled back into the pilot's seat. The food had done him some good. The chair didn't feel so alien now. It definitely wasn't designed with a human in mind, but it felt more comfortable than it had the first time he had sat in it. Paul smiled as he studied the console with its array of blinking lights and switches. Despite his grief, he was still amazed that the knowledge download from his Ambra, that he knew *the Specter* better than he'd known his laptop.

With a glance, he saw everything was in order. They were on course with a fully charged shields, weapons, and cloak system. Satisfied, he finally looked out the viewport at the rust-colored orb of Mars, half hidden by shadow as the ship approached it. A flash of movement across its surface made

Paul jump. He nearly sent the ship into an evasive maneuver until he realized it was Phobos making its rapid orbit around the planet. Paul looked for Deimos, the larger moon of Mars, but it was hidden behind the rapidly approaching planet.

Disengage cloak and perform passive scan.

Paul wanted to take in the view longer, but he didn't have time. With a sigh, he switched off the cloaking field and ran a quick passive sensor sweep. Within moments the combat map superimposed on the viewport changed with updated positions for the enemy fighters and warship.

Re-engage cloak. Analyzing data.

Paul could see the starfighters had given up finding *the Specter* in the area immediately surrounding Earth and had fanned out. One group would have caught their trail had they been breaking for the Gate again. The other two groups were still searching between the base ship and Earth. One flight group appeared to be meandering closer to a vector that might place Mars in their sensor field. The command ship had moved closer to Earth, but was still picking up speed.

Data analysis complete. Course corrections unnecessary for now.

"That's good news," Paul muttered.

Displaying flight path in your HUD. As soon as we pass the first marker, engage thrusters to full and keep us on course to the following markers.

A series of square outlines appeared along the edge of the dark side of the planet in his HUD.

"Won't they pick up our thrusters and come running?"

Only if you hit them too early or fail to shut down on my mark. The planet will block their sensors.

"Got it. Can you give me a five second warning for thruster burn?"

No problem.

"Good, let's go save some more people," Paul said. He felt a twang of pain. It felt good to be doing something instead of replaying the horror in his head, but it was still a reminder of what could go wrong.

The transport picked up speed as the Martian gravity pulled

the ship. A dark thought flashed in Paul's mind as he wondered what it would be like to let the planet's gravity take the ship and send it crashing into the surface. He shook the thought away, and his cheeks warmed with guilt.

Great, I'm going to hear all about suicidal ideation now from Zyp, he thought.

It surprised Paul when the Ambra let the thought go by without comment. He'd more than half expected a snarky potshot, at least.

The first marker was larger than he had assumed when they first appeared, and now it looked like a bright glowing box that filled most of his viewport.

5 seconds to thrust.

Paul disengaged autopilot and brought back manual control.

4 seconds.

Paul gripped the controls lightly, keeping his grip loose.

3 seconds.

He kept his sight on the marker as he gripped the throttle.

2 seconds.

He ignored the bead of sweat dripping down his nose.

1 second.

He held his breath as the marker streaked past the viewport.

Now.

Paul set the throttle to full and shifted towards the next marker. His stomach lurched as the inertia pushed him into his seat until the dampeners equalized. The planet went dark above him, and he saw Deimos rising over the dark horizon, reflecting the faint light of the sun. He wished he had time to watch it.

The ship passed through the second and third markers easily, but by the time they got to the fourth, the speed increase made Paul have trouble keeping the ship in the pathway. By the fifth, he had veered off to the side of the target square.

By the sixth marker he was getting off course, with the ship barely staying in the target area.

Paul missed the 7th marker entirely, passing closer to the

planet.

Course correct!

Paul eased up on the throttle and adjusted the course and passed through the 8th marker.

The loud ding of the kitchen timer Zyp loved made Paul cringe as he passed through the 9th marker.

4 seconds.

"Dammit Zyp, erase that noise from your memory!"

3 seconds.

The ship passed through the 10th marker.

2 seconds.

The ship barely made it through the 11th marker and Paul scrambled to line up the last, his movements frantic.

1 second.

Paul jerked as the transport passed right through the flowing line of the marker, and then he pulled the throttle to the off position just as the oven timer chimed brightly.

Cut thrust!

Deimos passed close above *the Specter* as it broke orbit, moving much faster than before.

"I missed one. Are we still on course?"

You missed two. And yes, we're close enough. I calculated a path that would get us there as long as you made half of the markers.

"You couldn't tell *me* that?!" He was shouting now, waving his hands in exasperation.

I could've, but I wanted to see how you'd do. It was a standard training exercise. We could have just used the autopilot. I'm surprised you didn't notice.

"Gah, didn't you learn enough about me already?!"

The longer we're bonded, the more I know about you and the more accurate my assessment. And the more I can help you.

"Well, what did you figure out about me now?"

The bright sound of the kitchen timer rang in his head again.

Congratulations. Between your performance with starfighters and bombers, and the slingshot

*** maneuver, you're now a Level Two pilot!***

Paul rubbed his hands roughly across his face, willing the tension away. It didn't work.

"I thought I told you to delete that noise! It makes me feel like I'm a batch of cookies!" Paul waved his hand in exasperation. "Well, go ahead. Tell me what being a Level Two whatever means so we can get back to planning this rescue!"

Chapter 24.

"Time to move." Edolit motioned her team to form up behind her. The break had done her some good, but she was still shaky on her feet as she stepped into the corridor.

Ka'ilk. Re-engage stim protocol.

The warm flood of hormone spread through her chest and fatigue faded from her body.

Stims engaged. I've analyzed the files you copied from the terminal. You need to see something.

We need to move, Nian. Can it wait?

I do not believe so.

Edolit motioned for Omaro and Ja'el to take up guard positions beside the recessed entry to a side hatch while she crouched down.

Okay, what do you have?

Job postings for a series of worlds for an organization called 'The Syndicate.' I found them highly irregular since none of the worlds are part of the Federation and no organization by that name exists in official records.

Show me.

Her HUD filled with a scrolling list of worlds, most of which she had never heard of. Hundreds of worlds in dozens of border systems. Beside them were numbers of duty postings. She picked a world at random - Skabe - and the list stopped scrolling. A drop-down menu of jobs appeared with start dates only a few standard weeks away. With a glance, she saw positions covering an array of resource collection jobs and manufacturing. Mining. Ore Processing. Chemical Extraction. Shipyard construction. Fleet officers. Administrative staff.

Is it like this for all worlds?

Yes, with some minor variation. Some appear to be mining and construction operations, others appear to be bio-resource extraction. Some worlds already have production output targets that include starfighters and border patrol light cruisers. Other worlds appear to be harvesting operations only.

Harvesting?

I infer it to be the Syndicate's designation for slaves.

Any other information about their plans?

There are other files referenced, but they did not appear to have been accessible by the terminal.

Captain Numoh would have access. Do we have a route to his personal office?

The list disappeared from view and her map updated with an alternative route outlined. The path took them in the bridge's direction at the center of the ship, with the Captain's quarters separated from the rest of the crew's.

Projected resistance?

Troop registry indicates a squad stationed on the bridge with multiple patrol routes surrounding it. It's unlikely that conflict can be avoided.

She pulsed the grim gray tone of concern. There was something bigger than the takeover of a single planet going on, and she needed to find out more. Her gut told her that the Gryx and the Syndicate they served were about to make their move. Between the list and the evidence she had already gathered, there was powerful evidence against the Gryx, but not enough to compel the Federation into action. They needed an obvious violation to turn the might of the Federation military against them. Even if the Resistance remained the only ones organizing against Gryx overreach and this

Syndicate, there would be information in Numoh's quarters they could use.

Any status on extraction?

Unknown.

The wail of Omaro's blaster made Edolit jump, and she swung around. The Scyllarian was in a relaxed position, the barrel of his blaster still smoking with ozone.

"Just a crewman. Only a matter of time before the cavalry shows up, though," Omaro said. He jerked his weapon slightly and fired again. A muffled gurgle from down the corridor let Edolit know he'd downed another Gryx.

"Noted. We're changing plans. We've got to get to the captain's quarters for intel, Priority One. Along the way we'll destroy anything that looks important."

With a tap of her Ambra screen, she sent the route to the members of the team. With a nod of his armored head, Omaro led them away.

***

They moved quickly, silent and alert. Ja'el swayed slightly, still feeling the effects of the suppressors, but she kept up with their pace. The wounded Grr'alis had a hard time keeping her weapon at the ready, but she hadn't been effective for anything more than cover fire since her rescue, anyway. With no time for concern, Edolit noted it and kept them moving. There was nothing she could do for her at the moment.

At one intersection, two startled Varanul turned the corner only to be shot by two quick reflexive shots from the dual blasters Omaro wielded. They were dead before they hit the floor and had no time to send out an alert. The close call made Edolit slow their pace and curse the bright, open design of the *Xyanthin-class* cruisers. The Gryx had always preferred bright spaces and smooth design, and the result was a ship design that left few shadowy nooks to hide in. If they got caught in the middle of a straightaway, the only cover they would have would be the recessed entrances of the occasional hatchway.

Fortunately, the ship was large, the few patrols they encountered were small, and the open design made it hard to set up defensive choke points. The troop complement on the vessel was stretched thin, trying to search for them on all decks. Edolit knew a majority of their force would focus on the hanger bay to block their escape, especially after she had discovered all escape pods were locked down.

The next patrol they encountered got off a couple of shots before being gunned down by concentrated fire from Edolit and Omaro. Edolit motioned for Omaro to drag the Varanul's bodies into the Captain's Quarters behind them. She pivoted to the side so he wouldn't see the wound she'd received, quickly covering it with a gelpak she'd taken from the medbay. He noticed her bright red pulse of pain when he finished. His maxillipeds twitched, but he locked the hatch without comment.

The captain's quarters were more cluttered than she expected. The Gryx prided themselves on their utilitarian minimalism and sense of order, but Numoh's walls were covered in an amalgam of artifacts from dozens of different cultures. Smaller pieces cluttered his desk as well. Some were trinkets found at any tourist's hovel but others were complicated works of art, but most were weapons. A rack of staffs, antique bolt throwers, and blades from ten different worlds were mounted behind his desk. Edolit growled, her skin pulsing the deep maroon of rage as she spotted her Honor Blade among them.

"Seal the door and keep your sensory enhance mode on. Let me know if you hear a patrol coming," she growled. The sight of her blade among the Captain's trophies ignited a deep, searing flame within her. "Ja'el..."

Edolit started when she saw Ja'el slumped down beside the desk, her back against the bulkhead. The Grr'alis stared at the charred bodies of the Varanul blankly, her pink skin faded and dripping with gray sweat, her breath heaving. She looked as if she would keel over at any moment. Omaro glanced down at Ja'el and then met Edolit's eyes as he took up a position against the door once it sealed.

"Ja'el, rest up, but be ready to move," Edolit said, moving towards the desk. Ja'el nodded weakly.

Nian, scan for terminals and datapads.

Located.

A large box outline inside the desk appeared on her HUD, along with two smaller devices in other drawers. Glancing at her blade, Edolit set her blasters on the desk and ripped open the compartments. Inside one was a larger quantum server hub with a mobile terminal. She left it in place and pulled the smaller datapads out of the center drawer first. One wasn't password protected. A cursory glance showed it was full of similar data to what she had already found in the terminals. The next pad was password protected.

Here we go.

Gingerly, she placed the pad on the desk and laid her left arm beside it. With a quick flick of her finger against the side of her Ambra, she opened its port panel, extended the data cable, and attached it to the datapad.

Run the decrypt program.

Scanning. Estimated decrypt time 3.75 minutes.

"Omaro, I need 5 minutes."

"You got it Commander, so far it's quiet out there."

While the decrypt ran, Edolit pulled out the mobile terminal and flicked on the screen. It showed an array of news and corporate headline feeds streaming from the Federation core worlds, but also had a local data feed open, showing system alerts for the ship. A quick glance at the alert feed made her curse.

"Brace yourselves. Looks like we tripped an alarm when we came in here. They've got two squads on their way. The ship is at max speed, course set for Earth, we're running out of time."

Chapter 25.

Paul was overwhelmed with the technology tree hovering in front of him, but he was closer to understanding how the Ambra helped him. The skill levels unlocked a series of related upgrades the device could perform. While downloading knowledge directly into his brain was possible for most anything, augmenting an existing skill worked different. Knowing the controls for the ship differed from having experience *using* them. Knowing something intellectually was different from experiencing it. The more Paul experience he gained, and the more he used his skills, the more the Ambra could augment him.

It took some explaining, but he thought he got it now. Zyp used the example of the difference between knowing the forms of a fighting style and being able to use them in a fight. One required thought and deliberate brain power, the other was instinctual and relied on muscle memory. The Ambra could download the knowledge of how to fight, but until he had *used* the knowledge, it couldn't augment his speed and agility. Without some practice, it couldn't make him fight the way Edolit had against the Varanul. With the case of his pilot's ability, the Ambra now had a good baseline of his abilities in that respect and could now increase his reaction time, focus, and accuracy.

Now he faced the decision of what upgrade would most help

the rescue. Like knowledge downloads, upgrades were spaced between levels to help prevent brain melt down and to allow for better integration. He could choose to play to his strength or make up for his weaknesses, or save them up for a later when he wasn't in the heat of battle and unable to spare the recovery time necessary for them.

He had time before final maneuvers, and he intended to use it to better their chances.

The tech tree had been expansive, with everything he could imagine that would affect each of his baseline skills and even more that he couldn't imagine. The entire concept made him wish he had played more role-playing games as a kid to prepare him. He resisted the urge to pour his upgrades into strength or athletics. He was a pilot. As fun as it sounded to gain super strength, it wouldn't help him.

In the end, he augmented Gunnery. He'd be in tight quarters during the rescue attempt, with little room to maneuver. Any edge to his accuracy would be worth it. Paul wondered if the augmentation would have made a difference against the bombers. The thought weighed on him until Zyp projected the image of the cruiser in front of him, the Ambra's way of distracting him from his own thoughts.

Paul cringed as he looked at the image of the *Xyanthin-class* cruiser hovering in the air. He'd originally asked to have a scale image of his transport projected beside the image for reference, but it had instantly sent him into a panic attack and he had Zyp remove it. The 500 meter long cruiser's heavy cannons, point defense lasers, and missile turrets made it a virtual fortress when compared to the tiny transport he was flying. His instinct told him to turn tail and run, to burn hard for Earth and hope he found a hole to hide in before the invasion.

But then I would let Edolit and her team down. They're counting on me. I have to make this work. The thoughts weighed on him, he'd been staring at the display for fifteen minutes as the ship sped ever closer to Jupiter and its many moons, hurling towards what Paul was coming to realize was most likely a certain death.

We may be in range to get a more accurate reading on the ship's position now. Would that help you grow a pair?

Paul groaned. The longer he had been bonded with Zyp, the more the intelligent device had picked up on the myriad of colloquial phrases and slang peppered throughout Paul's memory. Some of it was making him a little more comfortable with the voice in his head, made it sound a little more familiar. The rest was a catch-all of some of the most annoying phrases that had infected Paul's brain from the minefield of pop culture.

"Please delete that phrase from your memory banks and mine. It's awful," Paul muttered. He didn't think Zyp would listen to him, but he thought he'd give it a shot.

Okay.

"Wait, really?"

Since you asked nicely, sure. I don't understand it, anyway. What are you growing a pair of?

The sound of his own laughter surprised Paul. When was the last time he had done that? The past couple of days certainly had been tense. Laughter was a welcome relief from his exhaustion.

"Zyp, will you please delete that oven timer noise, now?"

Ding.

"Okay, now you're just mocking me with it."

Ding. Ding.

Paul gave up and looked at the cruiser again, going over what he knew, shaking his head and smiling. The moment of levity had helped, and he could look at the image without complete terror overtaking him. There was one hanger bay, likely mostly empty now that he had destroyed a squadron of bombers and lured the starfighters out to search for him. With Edolit loose, it would be heavily guarded, since they would assume she would try to commandeer whatever ship was left in the hanger to make her escape.

"Zyp, how effective is this ship against entrenched ground troops?"

The shields and hull can withstand most small

weapons' fire. If they have a mobile heavy cannons setup, they'd get through the shields eventually, though.

"Do you have a diagram of what the hanger looks like?"

Sure. It's approximate, but should give you an idea.

The diagram zoomed in and stripped away the outer hull. The hanger was crescent shaped, with a large holding bay in the center half circle and two angular launch sections wide enough for three of the bombers to leave the hanger in tandem on either side of the ship.

The hanger had two entrances, designed for quick deployment of the fighters on two fronts. Each entrance was nestled opposite each other in the hull in an indented grove in the design. The armored bow of the cruiser shielded the hangers from approach and allowed the fighters a microsecond to build up speed before they left the safety of the cruiser's shields. They angled hangers gave the cruiser a shark-like appearance, the hanger grooves like the gills behind its heavily armored, angular "head."

Unfortunately for Paul, it also limited the vector of approach. He'd have to approach from the rear half of the ship. The designers of the ship considered that, and to protect the hangers from approach by boarding parties, they had mounted multiple point defense cannons on either side to cover the approach vectors.

"So, I know I'll have to approach in cloak mode to avoid those defense cannons." Paul pointed to each of them, more for himself than Zyp. It helped him to talk things through sometimes, even to himself.

Correct. The transport could only handle a few direct hits from those cannons before the shields would collapse.

"And then once in the hanger, I'll have to take out an unknown number of entrenched troops," Paul grumbled. "Can you show me probable positions they might use to cover internal entrances to the hanger?"

I can give you a guess.

"That's better than nothing, do it."

The diagram placed several clusters of dots to show likely troop positions and extended cones to indicate where their fields of fire would be to cover the doors. The curve of the launch sections kept two clusters separated from each other by the bulkhead, but the other five groups had overlapping fields of fire.

"So I've got to take out as many fire teams as I can with no targeting reference except for what I can see with my own eyes?"

At least until you are within the hanger. After you'll need to disengage cloak to contact Edolit, anyway.

"Right, but by then they'll be diving for cover and calling for backup."

And alerting the starfighters.

"So we'll be holding position for an unknown amount of time until Edolit shows up, hoping the ground troops don't have a heavy cannon, and that we get out before starfighters arrive and box us in?"

That about sums it up.

"That's a lot of stuff out of our control to worry about." Paul's anxiety was growing more insistent. "Could we cut through the hull and pick up in another location?"

The hull is a meter thick, designed to resist direct laser fire and missiles. We don't have the cutting tools required.

"Crap. So the hanger is the only option."

Yes. I suggest a sensor scan to show starfighter positioning and check for messages from Edolit.

Paul hesitated. He could see Jupiter now, the bright light of the planet taking shape against the backdrop of stars. The glow of the warship's drive was visible, moving away from the planet. If they were scanning when he de-cloaked, they'd be out of options.

But they needed to have a better idea of what was happening.

"Okay, but I'm only going to run the scan for a couple of

seconds. Send Edolit an ETA for arrival so she can be en route to the hanger. The less time we have to hold the position the better."

Agreed. Data packet prepared. Ready when you are.

"Okay. Here goes nothing." Paul flicked off the cloaking device and gripped the controls, prepared to take evasive action if necessary. He counted to three and reactivated it. He kept his grip on the controls as he checked the combat map. The starfighters were still spread out, sweeping the area just inside of Martian orbit at this point.

The cruiser appears to be burning at max speed towards Earth, based on the limited sensor data.

The weight of the artificial gravity felt like it had increased as Paul sank into the pilot's seat. The cruiser was en route to finish the job the bombers had started. And there was nothing he could do. Panic tried to take over his brain, but he forced it down. He would save whoever he could, and right now that meant Edolit's team. Maybe together they'd come up with a way to cripple the ship.

He reminded himself there wasn't any chance the cruiser wouldn't be noticed by someone on Earth, especially not after a disaster like El Paso. The militaries had to be on high alert for something and have eyes glued to every satellite available. Surely they could get people to shelter and mount some sort of resistance, right? The thought comforted Paul enough to overcome his shock.

"Okay, calculate the best intercept course to bring us behind the cruiser with as few course corrections as possible. Calculate intercept time for any fighters that may have picked up our sensor scan. Any word from Edolit?"

She has freed two members of Specter team and is currently raiding the ship's data files. I flashed her our ETA, and she acknowledged pickup location.

"Well, we just have to hope for the best. If all else fails, I can do some damage inside that thing before we get taken out."

Chapter 26.

Numoh led the entire bridge security detail towards his quarters. The lurch of the ship's engines didn't make him miss a step. His entire career had been spent on large ships, from his time in the Federation fleet to now. It had all brought him to this point, and he wasn't about to let a small band of Resistance scum wreck his chance to bring his ship home to the core.

"Have Squads Three and Four reinforce the hanger. Squad Two will approach from C deck. We'll box them in from the other side." Numoh was casual in his commands, projecting utmost confidence for his subordinates. Inside, however, he was still raging. He should have seen this move coming. Of course the Hylian would attempt to recover her precious Honor Blade and attempt to discover anything she could from his private terminal. She was a spy, after all.

Her zeal for the truth would be her undoing. She would be trapped, and he could recover her precious Ambra.

The power of that tech was far more impressive than their preliminary reports had shown. Syndicate Leadership was obviously desperate to get their hands on it too. With the massive fleet they had built in secret, they already knew they had a chance against the might of the Federation, especially when the Federation's Sixth Fleet defects at the proper time. But with those Ambras augmenting their troops... they'd be unstoppable. The entirety of known space would be theirs to claim. The long heralded Gryx Empire would begin its dominance, and it would no longer need its shadow organization the Syndicate to cover up its dirty work.

First, he had to capture Edolit Vyn and force her to do his bidding. As protective as she was of her crew, he knew how to make her spill her secrets. Watching the scrawny Grr'alis being tortured had nearly broken that Scyllarian cretin, but he'd seen the glimmer in Vyn's eyes when he alluded to what he'd do. He had the utmost confidence that he could break her. He only wondered which member of her crew he would have to send out the airlock first.

The corridor outside his quarters was silent, save for the clattering of Varanul claws against the deck, loud against the soft steps of the Gryx crewman. In his periphery, Numoh noted the way the Gryx crewmen cowered behind the Varanul, their hands showing the slightest hint of shaking. He scowled, the visible fear a reminder of how much the Gryx had been relying on their vat-grown warriors for too long. After this mission was complete, he would have to double the training regimen for all crewmen to include more live-fire exercises.

Hanging back, he watched the Varanul calmly begin cutting through his hatchway with plasma cutters, unconcerned that they would be the first cut down. At least he could count on these creatures to do their jobs with unflinching resolve. Perhaps, after the Gryx fleet gets hardened in the coming battles, he would be able to depend on his crewman do perform as well.

Chapter 27.

Edolit grabbed her Honor Blade from the wall and set it on the desk beside her. The sounds of plasma cutters whirred through the hatchway. They didn't have long before the Varanul would burn through. She just hoped she had time to finish her mission.

Ja'el and Omaro had barricaded the door as much as they could with the contents of the Captain's quarters. Anything to slow the Varanul when they broke through. Edolit hoped to be long gone before then, but if not they had to block the doorway with enough bodies to bottleneck the assault.

While they worked, she set up the quantum terminal to receive the data. Her plan was simple. Since she couldn't trust the quantum network security to get the data to her people alone, she was going to make sure everyone had it. Whatever the Syndicate was planning would go out to all networks, agencies, militaries, corporations, and social hubs she could access, as well as the Resistance and Federation leadership. The Gryx would scramble to block and delete the files from the network, but it was nearly impossible to stop a leak of that magnitude from spreading once it was out there. Within seconds, hundreds of copies would be downloaded and forwarded throughout the entire Federation network, virtually guaranteeing that whatever they were planning would be exposed within minutes.

Then they could make a break for the hanger.

Ja'el had settled into her position next to the desk, partially covered by a side table she had turned over for a cover. Omaro had set up his own barricade on the other side, which would force the assailants to split their fire and give them all a slightly better chance. Edolit motioned Omaro over with her head and handed him the blade.

"Start cutting through to the deck beneath us. I'm almost done here," she said.

He grinned, his maxillae chittering with excitement. He'd always wanted to use her blade, but she'd never allowed it. He flicked the switch, and it hummed to life, casting its fuchsia glow over his carapace. The smell of melting metal soon filled the room as he eagerly set to work, slicing away at decking behind the desk. Edolit thought she heard him chattering happily to himself.

Message received from Zyp, ETA 15 minutes to Hanger.

"Fifteen minutes to pick up," she said with a smile and a teal pulse of gratitude. *I knew you'd come through.*

"We won't make it five," Ja'el muttered.

"Stow it, solider. We'll make it."

Decrypt complete. Beginning file transfer. Two minutes for complete copy download.

Upload all files to the network immediately, including all data from Earth scout mission. Rapid release as soon as you can. Edolit had already linked the terminal to the Ambra. She pulsed relief as she saw bursts of data streaming onto the screen.

Confirmed.

"Two minutes and we're out of here. How's that hole coming, Omaro?"

"I'm through this deck, starting on the one below. I'll be done in time, Commander."

The muffled sound of an explosion outside the door made Edolit grab her blaster and swing it towards the door. The top half of the door was glowing red, super-heated from a concentrated blast.

"Commander, they finally got thermal charges up here," Ja'el muttered.

"I see it. Next one will blow the door. Get ready to fire," Edolit growled. "Cut faster, Omaro."

"We're dead, Commander," Ja'el said, the barrel of her blaster shaking.

"We just have to hold a few more seconds. Get down that hole as soon as it's cut, Ja'el."

Ja'el's reply was lost in the wail of the thermal explosion tearing through the door. Molten gobs of slagged metal showered the room, but Edolit did her best to ignore them, firing blindly into the smoking corridor beyond.

Let me know the second you're done with the transfer, she ordered Nian.

Confirmed. Approximately 30 seconds.

She knew from experience that 30 seconds was an eternity in a close quarters firefight. Especially when she was the only one firing.

"Ja'el, fire now!" she shouted. A blast from her weapon sent a Varanul who had tried to rush the opening howling from the doorway with a searing wound in its arm. She fired randomly while she stole a glance towards the Grr'alis.

Ja'el was hunkered down behind her barricade with her remaining arm shielding her head, muttering to herself. She had twisted into a small, trembling ball, her species' dexterity allowing her body to fold in on itself. Edolit wasn't sure what they did to torture her, but her friend had been broken more completely than she'd thought.

"Omaro, finish that hole and get Ja'el down it now!" Edolit shouted, taking down a Varanul that had taken up a crouching position across the hall. Return fire was streaming through the hole as the Varanul outside sent unaimed microbursts of fire through the door.

"Just a ...," Omaro shouted back. Edolit heard a large boot kicking metal behind her, and the Scyllarian shouted triumphantly. "Got it, Commander!"

The hum of her Honor Blade stopped, and the welcome tone of Omaro's blaster joined hers as he rushed to Ja'el.

"C'mon, time to move," he said to the Grr'alis, continuing to shoot towards the doorway. He tried to nudge her to motion, but she trashed blindly at him, kicking and screaming in terror.

A bright, searing pain surged through Edolit as a blaster bolt slammed into her left shoulder. Her vision blurred and the force of the impact wrenched her torso, wrenching her arm behind her. The data cable pulled from the terminal as she shot the Varanul who had appeared in the doorway.

Data connection lost. Heavy damage sustained. Initiating Healing Protocol. Display Status?

Negative. Cancel Healing Protocol. Put all energy towards file transfer when reconnected.

"Cover me, Omaro." The sounds of his blasters filled the room immediately. She could always count on him to react quickly.

With one last shot towards the door, she dropped her blaster on the desk and fumbled with the cable. The blood streaming down her arm made it slippery, but she reinserted it with some cursing. The desk took more and more direct hits from blasters, its ferroucarbon frame crumbling. They were close to being overrun.

"Got it! Get her out of here!" Edolit shouted as she grabbed blasters in both hands and sent bolts streaming towards the door. Her left arm was hindered by the data cables and unable to aim, so she used it for random cover fire. She could barely move it due to the shoulder wound, anyway. She aimed more carefully with her free hand. Her instincts screamed for her to have Nian augment her reaction time and targeting skills, but knew it would slow down the data transfer. The countless hours spent practicing with blasters at the range without augmentation served her well now.

Omaro's loud grunts from carrying Ja'el to the opening reassured Edolit as she fired. She would leave no one behind, not this time, even if it cost her life. Her mission was almost complete, the Syndicate's plans would be leaked, and all that mattered to her now was protecting her people.

Ja'el's muffled scream behind her was followed by the

clattering of plastoid cases hitting the deck. The sound of Omaro's blaster joined hers again.

"You're bleeding bad," he grunted.

"I'm fine. Get out of here, and get her moving towards the hanger," she growled. She ducked, narrowly avoiding a blast, and downed the Gryx crewman that had sent it her way.

"But…"

"That's an order. I'm right behind you."

"Yes, Commander. I'll have this waiting for you, make sure you're there to claim it." Omaro scooped up her blade and disappeared down the hole.

The seconds ticked by, and blaster fire increased all around her. She took glancing near misses to the arms and chest, but she barely registered the pain. Her focus was unwavering. Her battle prowess had taken over, and she dealt out death accordingly. All that mattered to her was holding her ground.

Nian's calm voice broke through her battle rage. **Data transfer complete.**

Good job. One more thing to do. Edolit felt a surge of relief, followed by the quick pang of grief. She knew Nian could see her thoughts.

I concur. It's been an honor, Commander.

You too, Nian. Command Override Code 1-327. Set time for 15.

Self-destruct Command Confirmed. Goodbye Edolit.

Goodbye, Nian.

She kept firing, hitting the Ambra's quick release button with her free hand. The device ejected from its mounting and severed nerve circuits instantly, and the flat device came off in her hand. She gasped at the sudden void she felt as Nian's consciousness disconnected. A barrage of pain buffeted her a microsecond later, her pain receptors no longer blocked by the Ambra.

Fifteen small red dots appeared on the screen, pulsed yellow, and began disappearing.

Edolit tossed the Ambra on the desk, grabbed her blaster, and dove towards the hole in the deck. She hoped the captain's quarters were full of Varanul before the device exploded, but she'd settle for it covering their escape. Even if it just blocked the way, it would give her and her team a chance.

She landed on her feet with a harsh jolt of pain as she hit the deck. Stumbling, ran straight for the corridor, barely registering the storage room she landed in. Omaro was waiting outside the door, holding up Ja'el with one arm and a blaster at the ready with the other. Edolit pulsed the pattern of disappointment when she saw Ja'el's head slumped down, unconscious.

"Move!" she shouted while she took up position on Ja'el's other side and pulled them down the corridor, barely registering the searing pain in her shoulder as she strained to carry her pilot to safety. The metal bolts and fibers of her empty Ambra housing made her forearm burn and throb as it pressed against Ja'el's back.

They got a few meters away before the room behind them exploded with a rushing wave of heat and kinetic force. They staggered and struggled to keep upright, but managed to keep moving. Edolit spared a moment to thank Gryx ship designers for placing the bridge and captain's quarters in the center of the ship. She couldn't have pulled that stunt on decks closer to the hull without risking depressurization.

"That'll buy us a little time, but we need to get off this level, now. You've got the comms, Omaro. Alert Zyp and tell me if they send us any word." Edolit barked the command more harshly than intended, the pain of her wounds now dominating her mind. She felt weighed down. The sudden absence of the stims and pain blockers that had been coursing through her system was a shock. She hadn't realized how much energy the Ambra was expending in keeping her going. Without them, she was sluggish and weakened, running on willpower alone.

"Yes Commander. We've got to get you patched up as soon as we can," Omaro said.

"We don't have time for that, move."

"If we don't, I'll have to carry two of you. Plus, you're leaving a nice gory trail for them to follow," he said, nodding towards the blood dripping from her multiple wounds.

"Fine." She stopped and ripped open the last gelpak she'd tucked into her belt. She ripped it in two and slapped half over her shoulder wound, and the other on a deep gash she'd gotten from the jagged edges of their escape hatch. It didn't cover both wounds completely, but it would hold, at least for a little while.

"That should do for now. The rest can wait, I'll be fine," she said.

Omaro's maxillipeds chittered in disapproval, but he let it drop. He'd worked with her long enough to know that was the most he'd get out of her until they were further away.

Edolit took up position beside Ja'el's limp form again. After a few meters of stumbling, they found a rhythm that kept them moving steady, despite her deepening fatigue.

"I didn't think she'd ever break like this," Edolit said. She silently cursed herself for not keeping her away from those pain meds. She'd obviously taken far too much and had nodded out, even with the protective nanotech of the Ambra cleaning her system.

A haunted expression passed over Omaro's face, his maxillae twitching.

"They made me watch. Numoh knew it was the only thing they could do that might make me talk," he said. "He didn't just take her arm. He had the Varanul take it one sliver at a time. The captain... the bastard enjoyed it. He waved each finger, each slice of her in front of my face and remind me that only I had the power to stop it."

Edolit didn't know what to say. She'd experienced torture before, even some at Numoh's hands, but nothing remotely as gruesome as that. It seemed as if he was only getting started with her.

"Problem was, she didn't pass out until the elbow. So... I don't blame her for breaking," he said. The hard edged Scyllarian had never shown much emotion. When he'd first joined the team, she'd thought he was gruff. It had only taken a single mission to learn he was more emotional than she gave him credit for. He kept it to himself because it was hard for other species to read the subtle movements of the maxillae and chitin plates of his face, and he knew the crew didn't understand. Edolit could hear anguish deep in the wavering pitch of his voice.

"We'll get her home, Omaro."

"I know. And after that, I'm going to make them pay," he said. His voice filled with an icy darkness Edolit had never heard in his voice before. The sound sent a chill down her spine. Part of her hoped she wasn't around to see what he would do.

Chapter 28.

"Well, how much time does the ship need to target the turrets?" Paul said in exasperation.

Seconds, but they're sensors are more powerful, they'll be tearing into our hull by then.

Paul was convinced he could stop or limit the amount of damage the cruiser could do to his world, somehow. Now that the pick up plan had been decided, the idea to destroy the cruiser's laser turrets had captured Paul's attention, and he couldn't let it go.

"What about using visual targeting? Staying cloaked but taking out the cannons without the computer?"

The heavy lasers would be easy to target, they are on rotating blisters to maximize their effective field of fire. The point defense lasers would be too small to spot easily. Plus, you forget they are all protected by the cruiser's particle shields, Captain Perceptive.

Paul slumped in his chair, the helplessness pressing on his chest. He felt good about his chances to save Edolit and her team, at least about the things he could control about the plan. There was little more he could do to save his world, though. The cruiser's weapons wouldn't cause the mass devastation that the bombs would have, but he knew it could still exact a terrible amount of damage, with little hope of a response from Earth. From orbit, it could leisurely destroy military bases, power grids, communications satellites, and fuel refineries that would bring the planet to a grinding, chaotic halt.

It might not be the destruction of humanity the Syndicate seemed to want, but it would bring the planet to its knees all the same. All he could do about it was rescue Edolit's team and get them to the Gate. He hoped they could return with reinforcements in time to save some of his world.

I'm sorry Paul. You've done all you can.

"Thanks, Zyp. It's just...," Paul trailed off. He didn't know really what to say. What can anyone say to the destruction of an entire world? To losing the last family he had left. To never getting to say goodbye.

I know. It sucks.

"Really? That's the best you can come up with?"

It sucks, a lot? I don't know, I'm used to being an asshole. Not trying to make someone feel better.

Paul managed a laugh. "Thanks for trying, at least." He was surprised to find that he felt a little better. He glanced out at the viewport. Jupiter was passing by now, the great swirling storm raging in its clouds and a myriad of small moons dancing around it. Paul wished he had time to take in these majestic sights in the solar system without the sense of impending doom.

Perhaps I'll get to someday if I make it through the next hour, he thought.

He sighed and closed down the HUD display of the cruiser diagram. He'd cause as much damage as he could from the inside, but he had to get there first.

"Okay, Zyp, let's go get your people."

Our people. You're part of the team now.

Paul smiled. "Okay then. Let's go get our people."

***

The cruiser was picking up speed as its mass moved further away from Jupiter's gravity well. Already moving much faster than the massive battleship, it made Paul feel like he was hurling towards his own doom at an ever increasing speed. His stomach churned, even though the cruiser still looked small against the sea of stars. The vast distances of space still felt unreal to him. It was hard to accept the tiny gray cruiser in the distance, glowing brightly in Jupiter's light, would dwarf an entire city block by the time he was next to it.

And he was about to fly into its belly.

He tried his best to steady his shaking hands as he punched the final navigational commands into the computer. The sudden flip of the ship and controlled burn was going to be more precise than the best pilot in the galaxy could pull off and hit their target. Since he knew he was nowhere in the same league as an Ace pilot, Paul hadn't even questioned it when Zyp had displayed the commands he needed to put into the computer. He trusted the Ambra's math and knew it would get him where they needed to be. Paul would have to do the rest once they got there.

You'll have to reverse thrusters right before we enter that hanger, or we'll crash.

"Got it, don't crash," Paul muttered.

And don't de-cloak until we're inside the hanger, otherwise those cannons will fry us.

"I know, I know," Paul said. As much as he'd love to know where those starfighters were, he knew the immediate threat of the point defense cannons was more pressing.

And don't destroy any hatches to the hanger until we know where they'll come from.

"I got it, Zyp! What's the matter, are you nervous?"

Aren't you?

"Well, yeah, but I'm human. I'm supposed to be nervous before I fly towards a battleship in a tin can!"

Don't be so speciesist; of course I get nervous! Any mildly self-aware being would be terrified right now! Especially with a human flying!

"Oh." Paul had always assumed the Zyp's attitude was an aspect of its programming. Some source code meant to make K'tal feel more in tune with it. He'd never even considered that the personality had genuine feelings. "Sorry, Zyp."

It's fine. I didn't expect a hairless ape to understand all this stuff right away, anyway.

"Fair enough," Paul said. It seemed unlikely that the Ambra

had showed its vulnerability for his benefit, but it made him feel better. Having a voice in his head should have made him feel crazy, but in reality it made the emptiness of space much less lonely.

It's almost time.

Paul felt anticipation pulse through him. He took a last look at the massive planet, with its beautiful swirling clouds of gas and raging storms. No matter what happened, it comforted him to know he had seen things no human had seen in person. He'd grown up on images of these wonders, but none did them true justice.

"Okay. I'm ready," he said. With a loud pop, he cracked his knuckles and gingerly placed his hands on the throttle and controls. He tried to relax while he waited for the navigational computer to make the maneuver. He thought about having Zyp give him a countdown, but decided it would only make him more anxious. Instead, he focused on his breath and surrendered; it was all out of his control for now.

Suddenly, the planet and the sea of stars spun wildly as the nose micro-thrusters engaged and flipped the ship. The inertial dampeners had no time to adjust, and Paul's vision blurred. His stomach turned under the wild change in force exerted on his body, and he closed his eyes to keep himself from vomiting until the forces calmed. The cruiser hovered in front of him, its drive plume bright against the starry tapestry, still moving away from *the Specter*. His stomach lurched again as the main thrusters engaged. The cruiser moved away more slowly as the transport's primary drive overcame the ship's momentum. Paul felt the deck shudder beneath his feet as conflicting forces fought for dominance.

For a brief moment, the ship came to a stop as it overcame the momentum of its previous trajectory. With a quick burst of full burn, *the Specter* surged towards the cruiser. The thrusters shut down almost immediately, the ship's target speed and trajectory achieved.

The rest was up to Paul.

Bright red flashes of light came coursing from the side of the cruiser in small bursts, and streaking towards the space the transport had occupied.

Damn, those gunners were on high alert! Paul resisted the urge to jerk the controls and pull them away from the laser fire as it streaked past them.

The lasers were firing in short bursts, each turret firing in different directions.

They appear to be firing randomly. Their computers have been unable to calculate trajectory for us yet.

"Yet?!" Paul's panic made his voice crack like a pubescent boy. The ship was enormous in the viewport, and his sense of its scale was making him rethink a lifetime of choices.

Prepare for reverse thrust!

Laser fire saturated the space ahead of the ship, as the gunners calculated *the Specter* was heading for the hanger bay. A brilliant flash of red streaked past the viewport, and Paul cringed, his eyes closing reflexively. The near-hit left streaks in his vision when he opened them, but he was happy to be alive to see them. The cruiser's hull and the dull glow of the hanger bay quickly took his attention back.

Now!

His heart leaped into his throat as he realized he'd lost focus. Panicked, he jerked the throttle forward to full reverse thrust. The sudden force against the ship made him lurch forward in his seat, but the straps held him tight. The ship slowed as it slipped through the haze of the energy shields surrounding the hanger. Paul still had to jerk the ship to the side to keep from hitting the inner wall of the launch tube. His maneuver kept them from hitting the side head on, but he had overcompensated. The ship scraped against the opposite wall of the tube before he could recover control. Red warning icons flashed across the display, but he didn't have the chance to check them. His focus was on the squad of surprised Varanul, turning and leveling blasters at the roar of invisible engines bursting into the hanger.

As the ship slowed, he lined up the first group of baffled Varanul in his crosshairs and squeezed the trigger. Twin streams of laser fire tore into the group, caught on the wrong side of a barricade. The ones that survived the onslaught tumbled to the ground from the sudden explosions around them and scrambled for cover.

The sight of Varanul being vaporized or torn apart under his first burst of fire shocked Paul with its gory violence. Somehow, destroying bombers and fighters had been easy for him. The destruction he saw was to an inanimate object, and it gave him a sense of separation between himself and the life he had taken. There was no such separation for him now. He was forced to watch the full, destructive power of his lasers as he swept them along the barricade the Varanul hid behind. Orange blood sprayed onto the decking as he vaporized their cover and sent fragments of metal tearing into their bodies. He was glad he couldn't see what the ship's drive was doing to their bodies as he passed.

The gore sickened him until he thought about the hundreds of thousands of people that had been murdered on Earth. Anger tightened his focus. Grimly, he kept firing as he engaged the grav-coils and cut the throttle with his free hand. The ship hovered above the deck, but stopped its forward movement.

Using micro-thrust, Paul lined up another group of entrenched Varanul pelting his forward shields with small blaster fire and flicked off the cloaking field. The Varanuls' laser fire became more concentrated as *the Specter* appeared, no longer a wavering force field hovering above the deck, but a solid target to focus on. A quick burst from the laser cannons sent the fire team scattering. Paul's targeting skills showed enough improvement from his upgrade to make his mind boggle at the difference.

Paul had expected Edolit and her team to be pinned down in a firefight in the hanger, waiting for him by this point. *I guess I was finally early to something for once,* he thought with a flash of satisfaction. He glanced at the red warnings displayed across the screen and then turned away. He wasn't worried about minor hull scraping at the moment.

"Zyp, tell them we're here and let me know if I can take out any of these entrances. And warn me if those starfighters are in the neighborhood, wouldja?" He was surprised at how focused he had become now that they were inside the ship.

Already pinged their location and sent evac code. They are closest to this entrance.

Paul's combat display updated with a bright green icon over an entrance to the hanger. With a glance he saw two groups of Varanul around the entrance, and three more clusters covering separate entrances closer to the launch bay on the other side of the ship. Remnants of the other two fire teams that had survived his initial attack joined the entrenched groups in peppering his shields with laser fire. The small weapons had little hope of breaking through his shields, at least in the short term.

"Okay, I'll take out these other entrances before they bring in something with more firepower." Paul swung the ship around to target the entrance opposite him.

Before he got there, a mass of Varanul carrying large shoulder-mounted cannons and gangly looking aliens in prim uniforms and oversized heads swarmed through the doors and scattered. Paul fired reflexively and cut down two before he blasted apart the doorway in a concentrate barrage of fire. He fired until the ceiling decking collapsed down into the corridor beyond and blocked the entrance. He scanned to see where the new soldiers had ended up, vaguely wondering if this new species was responsible for the proliferation of the black-eyed gray aliens that permeated pop culture. Heavy impacts splashed against the shielding as the remaining Varanul with the heavy cannons began opening fire.

A gruff voice with a strange, chittering echo chimed loudly from his Ambra. "We're on the way, kid. Just hold off for a couple minutes. We've got injured."

"Edolit?" Paul said, confused. He ignored the heavy cannon fire and swept the ship around towards the next entrance, trying to keep from getting swarmed. He was firing constantly now, trying to cause as much damage as possible, burning through bulkheads and vaporizing any equipment he saw.

"This is Omaro. Edolit's here. She had to engage her Ambra's self-destruct. Sounds like things are hairy out there," the chittering voice said.

"I'm working on it. Just get here quick, starfighters are inbound," he shouted. He was tearing apart the flight deck and sending bodies of Varanul and the gray aliens scattering through the air, trying to cause as much chaos as possible. "Zyp, make sure they get to the correct evac point and feed them enemy positions. Omaro, I'll get the ship as close as I can and clear the way."

"Copy that. Just leave some for me. Omaro out."

He tried to target another Varanul and missed, burning a hole in the bulkhead behind it. Paul glanced at his shields and saw that the heavier cannons and rifles the new troops were carrying were eating away at his shield strength.

"Don't have much choice," Paul grumbled, and kept firing.

Chapter 29.

Captain Numoh ignored the ringing in his auditory canals as he stormed back to the *Wildfire*'s bridge. Flanked by two Varanul of the bridge guard, he sent the remaining members to reinforce the hanger. At least, the few that had survived Edolit's explosion. The rest of the search teams were converging on the various routes in between his quarters and the hanger. Captain Numoh shouldn't have been surprised by the attempted infiltration of his office, but the sudden destruction of his entire bomber wing had been... distracting.

For a moment, he had been worried Edolit and her overly loyal team would attempt some plan to scuttle the ship, taking the lives of his entire crew with them to their doom. However, the tenacity he had witnessed the Commander exhibit in order to retrieve her Honor Blade and to protect the lives of her people convinced him she meant to commandeer the shuttle in the hanger. The occasional crewman she'd left alive, trapped in quarters along their path, told him she sought to avoid death whenever possible.

He'd make her regret that weakness.

He still sent some of his remaining armed troops to lock down or guard the more sensitive areas of the ship, just in case. When he cleaned up this debacle, he would be sure to push for increased security personnel on all ships of the Syndicate fleet, as well as monitoring cameras for all parts of the ships besides the security corridor. He'd already ordered the execution of the crewman who'd been ignoring his duty to watch the security feed when she escaped.

The bridge door slid open, and he walked through without slowing his pace. The crewmen at their stations looked up at him, their eyes wide with terror.

Something has happened..., Numoh thought.

"Commander Keul, report!" He met the gaze of the officer that served as his second in command. The normally hard-edged Gryx looked a sickly gray, and Numoh felt a deep, sinking feeling in the pit of his dual stomachs.

"A cloaked ship just entered the hanger bay. I've recalled all starfighters and routed all available troops to take it." The old officer hesitated. Something in his voice was off. Something bigger was happening, Numoh could see it in the Gryx's eyes.

"What else has happened?" Numoh was curious at what could evoke such a response from the normally unfazed secondary officer.

"Fleet Admiral Hya has requested immediate conference with you. Shall I transfer her to your private terminal?" Commander Keul's voice was grave.

Something very terrible has happened. Normally, he'd take all fleet command calls in his private quarters. That wasn't an option. He had to take this in front of the bridge crew.

"No. I'll take it at the comm station. The prisoners destroyed my terminal." He left out that they had destroyed his entire office. He motioned the comm station crewman aside and punched in his command code, willing his hands to stay steady.

The calm but stern face of Fleet Admiral Hya appeared on the screen in front of him and he began immediately reciting the proper greeting for someone of her rank.

"It is an honor...," he began, but her sharp voice cut him off.

"Explain yourself. Now."

Numoh looked up, aghast at the breech of protocol, his mind racing. The young Gryx Admiral was always fierce, but he could see now that she bristled with barely contained rage. Something terrible has happened for sure.

"I am hunting down three escaped prisoners on my ship. Concerning for sure, but nothing that should waste your valuable time," he said, forcing his voice to stay steady. Her forcefulness and dismissal of proper decorum concerned him.

"Ah. Your first mistake is that you should not have prisoners to begin with. My standing order is to execute all members of the Resistance!" She glowered at him for a moment, and he found himself thankful she was only scolding him from a screen.

"I saw an opportunity to retrieve technology I believe to be vital to our efforts." His protest felt flimsy even as he spoke.

"You saw an opportunity to enrich your standing, you mean! You disobeyed a direct order. That's reason enough to have you removed," Fleet Admiral Hya growled.

Numoh knew he had no defense, and so he offered none. "Yes, Admiral. I apologize."

"The second mistake might cost us decades of careful planning. That I cannot forgive," she said. Her voice was icy now, and it sent terror tingling up his spine.

"I know I ordered the attack on Earth early, but it was the only way to hide our plans when their transport escaped," he stammered.

"You don't know. Do you, Captain Numoh?"

"Know what?"

Fleet Admiral Hya's eyes narrowed into black slits.

"You are as reckless as you are a fool. That prisoner decrypted your personal files and uploaded them to the quantum network. Everything we have worked for has been laid bare for the entire Federation to see."

Numoh paled to a sickly white.

"I see you are smart enough to know the gravity of what has transpired. Now, instead of a carefully orchestrated expansion of the resources of our new Empire with the quiet takeover of backwater worlds, we find ourselves in a war."

Numoh felt guards move in behind either side of him.

"Captain Keul, please have Private Numoh report to the blockade in your hangar bay," she snarled. She leveled her gaze back at Numoh. "Now, Private Numoh, bring me the head of this Edolit Vyn or die trying. If you fail, I will personally place every member of your brood out the airlock like you should have done to your captives."

Numoh felt two heavy hands slam down on his shoulders. He spun wildly to see two members of the bridge guard gripping him. Captain Kuel grimly tore the captain's seal from Numoh's uniform and placed it on his own, avoiding Numoh's gaze. With a stiff gesture, he motioned for the guards to escort Numoh to the hanger. Numoh was in a state of shock as they dragged away him from the screen.

Captain Kuel turned to the screen and saluted. "Orders, Admiral?"

"Continue your assault on the planet. Get me its surrender within the cycle. I have the troop transport Harrier and cruiser Harvester en route to reinforce your position before the Federation or the Resistance can send their own forces."

"Yes, Admiral. It will be done," Captain Kuel said with as much confidence as he could muster. This wasn't the first time he had seen a figure in command striped of rank during his career, but he hadn't expected to be the one promoted because of it. The prospects made him bristle with anxious energy.

"See that it does," she said. The corner of her lip curled up into a snarl before she disappeared from the screen, the connection severed.

Captain Kuel walked over to Numoh and stopped in front of the stricken former captain. Kuel unholstered his sidearm and held it out for his former leader. The weapon had been in his family for decades and had always served him well.

"Here Cap..., Private, go get Vyn's head. Succeed so they may put you on an ore hauler," Captain Kuel said.

Numoh looked down at the weapon and shook his head, motioning to the guard's heavy Bl-66 pulse rifle instead. "I'll need something a little more powerful to take her down," Numoh said as he took the guard's weapon. "Thank you Captain Kuel."

The color was returning to Numoh's ashen features. Somehow, he felt a sense of relief at the loss of his command.

Only one thing remained, the most simple of all the things he had worried about for years. Kill or be killed. He only had to get that tenacious Hylian in his sights.

Then, finally, he would be free, and he would be happy to disappear.

Chapter 30.

"Back!," Edolit shouted as she reflexively blasted the crewman who had appeared from a side corridor.

Omaro blocked Ja'el's limp form with his body as they retreated to a nearby hatchway. He howled in pain as a blaster bolt burned through his side plate for his troubles. The Scyllarian oozed fluid from a half dozen wounds, his Ambra having trouble keeping up with healing the damage. The damage made him unsteady on his feet, but he kept using his chitin plates to shield the rest of his team.

Edolit let the limp body of the Grr'alis lean against Omaro's side and crouched, using Omaro's armor as cover as she reached around and shot the remaining Varanul pursuing them. She held her weapon at the ready for a moment. Smoke and the smell of ozone rose from its super-heated barrel; she expected more of the snarling beasts to pour out toward them. Edolit scrambled back to help carry Ja'el.

"Are you injured, Omaro?" Her initial thought was to request his health status from her Ambra. *It's going to take some time to get used to command without Nian's input.*

"I'll live," he said, his voice flat. "Come on, we've got to get moving. The kid is having a tough time in the hanger, they were ready for him."

"And he's never done anything like this before," she said.

Regret washed over her. She glanced at Ja'el, unconscious

from a head wound or overdose of pain meds, she couldn't tell. Her regret only worsened. She wondered how many more innocent beings would be dragged into fighting for their homes by the Gryx and their Syndicate. It weighed on her in the best of times, seeing beings she had recruited dying or snapping under the pressures of the shadow war. It shouldn't be their responsibility; none of them should be the ones fighting. The Federation was supposed to be the ones out here. They were supposed to protect all beings like they claimed, not just the enriched ones of the core worlds.

She hoped getting her proof of the Gryx's goals of domination out to the public would finally spur the Federation to action. It would expand the conflict away from the back alleys of border worlds, sending it deep into the core of the Federation. She worried sometimes, if it had been too long since the Federation had been forced to defend itself. Did it have enough will left to fight for itself, or had it rotted through to its core?

"You okay, Commander?" Omaro asked.

She smiled and forced a blue pulse of calm to flash across her face. "Just ready to get off this ship."

Ja'el let out a murmur and jerked in the beginning stages of waking.

"Almost there, just around this corner. The kid is trying to clear the area around the exit. Zyp says they are taking a lot of fire but they're not taking damage so far." Omaro came to the corner and paused. He poked his head around and jerked back as a hail of blaster fire splashed against the wall across from them. "Ka'ilk, they've got the entrance barricaded!"

"Show me!" Edolit growled.

Before Omaro could activate his display, blaster fire splashed above her head, and she dropped reflexively. Two Varanul were taking aim from the hallway ahead, trying to flank them while they were pinned down at the intersection. A flurry of shots from her blaster sent one falling backwards onto the deck before it could get another shot off. Omaro's return fire neatly burned out the other's center eye and it dropped in a heap next to its brethren.

"What? Where are we?" Ja'el weak voice was barely audible over the blaster fire, and the familiar hum of *The Specter's* engines in the hanger.

Omaro released his grip around Ja'el, and Edolit helped the Grr'alis to the ground and pressed her back against the wall. The sound of a second blaster rang out above them as Omaro drew another weapon and started firing.

"We're pinned down here, Commander. What's the play?" The Scyllarian's chittering voice was strained but controlled. He'd stand his ground as long as she needed him to.

Ja'el's remaining arm reached out towards Edolit's wounded shoulder. "Go. Leave me. I'll blow the corridor behind you," she said weakly. She raised her arm to show the self-destruct sequence already set into her Ambra with a resigned nod.

"No, we're not leaving you, don't you hear the ship? We're almost home." Edolit looked up to Omaro, "Send her your tactical display."

Omaro didn't give a verbal confirmation, but a combat map projected in the air above Ja'el's, sent by his Ambra while he kept up the cover fire. She glanced at the positions of the enemies behind the barricade and flanking from the side corridor. She knew what to do and handed one of her blasters to Ja'el.

"Here, watch his back until I get back. And be ready to move." She patted Ja'el's slender shoulder and stood, drew her blade from its scabbard, and flicked it to life.

The sound of blaster fire stopped as Omaro took out the last of the flanking Varanul. The gentle whir of Edolit's vibrating blade filled the surrounding air, and Omaro turned in surprise. His chest plates had taken a couple direct hits, and she saw he was barely staying on his feet as his Ambra struggled to keep him patched up. He couldn't handle much more.

"No, you can't. You're injured, Commander." He tried to push her back, frantic. She knocked his hand away.

"Then keep them pinned down until I'm on top of them," she growled. She tested her arm with a quick swipe of her blade and winced. Her shoulder wound was worse than she expected. She switched her hands, putting her blaster in the one she could barely hold up, and her blade in her non-dominant hand. She wasn't as skilled at the blade with that hand without the augmentation of the Ambra, but it would have to do.

"But..."

"That's an order. Just like on Triton IV. Three." She pulled the blaster at the ready next to her head, switched her blade to a backhand grip, and nodded to him. The blade's glow cast a fuchsia glow on the back of her stained jumpsuit.

"Two," he said, with a quick glance to the power packs meters on his blasters.

"One, go." She blindly fired her blaster towards the entrenched Varanul and winced as the heat of their return fire showered her hand with molten metal. A microsecond later, Omaro surged across the gap of the intersection, firing wildly with both blasters. The Varanul ducked or shifted their aim towards the new target and gave her the distraction she needed.

Wishing she had her Ambra more than ever, Edolit raced towards the barricade, firing rapidly. She wasn't worried about hitting anything, just keeping them pinned down. She guessed at their positions, once again realizing how much she relied on the Ambra's tactical data, and aimed her sprint to the left of a cluster. The short distance of the corridor felt warped in her mind, like it would never end. Hurried return fire bounced around her as they took snap shots towards her. The hum of her blade held at the ready behind her gave her the confidence she needed. She was born for moments like this.

Then she was upon them.

With all the strength she could muster in her burning legs, she dove over the barricade head first, blindly sweeping her blade to the right with her backhand grip. The swipe cut cleanly through a Varanul's skull. The creature slumped over onto its squad mate from the force of her momentum as she sailed past.

She tucked at the last moment and landed with a quick roll. When she felt the ground under her feet, she blindly kicked back and sent her body hurling back towards the barricade.

Hurried blaster bolts filled the space she had just occupied, narrowly missed her. She fired blindly towards the left, her shoulder screaming in pain at the angle. Her pain was rewarded with the angry howls as some of her blasts hit their mark. As she crashed back against the barricade, her backwards momentum drove her blade into the chest of a Varanul.

The gurgling sound of its howl let her know she had pierced its lung. The Varanul flailed desperately before she could gather strength to move. Edolit screamed as it battered her left side, and she felt her fractured ribs snap. Wheezing, she kept her grip on her blade as she fell forward, her momentum tearing the beast's chest open while she fell. The creature's gurgling howls ceased. She landed with a sickening thud and shock-waves of pain coursing through her. She looked up at the last Varanul, frantically leveling its weapon at her.

Before she could move, a blast from close range rang out, and the Varanul's head jerked to the side from the force of the impact. Reflexively, its death rattle jerked the pulse rifle's trigger, and a blast tore through the deck next to Edolit's chest. Searing droplets of metal splashed against her side, burning through her jumpsuit. Another microsecond and the creature would have gotten her.

"Took you long enough," she wheezed. She tried to get up, but collapsed onto the cool deck instead. She could hardly breathe, and she wondered if her cracked ribs had pierced her lung. The whine of *The Specter's* engines outside the open hatchway behind her comforted her. She'd done it.

"Commander!" Omaro's voice were panicked. She imagined she looked terrible between her own wounds and the orange Varanul blood splashed all over her. He began to climb over the barricade.

"No, I'll be okay. Go. Get Ja'el and tell Paul we're right inside the exit." The hum of her blade quieted, and she let it fall to the deck. He hesitated. For a moment she thought she would have to scold him, but his face disappeared. She let her head roll and pressed her cheek against the deck. The cool ferroucarbon felt wonderful against her cheek. She'd never felt so tired, and wanted nothing more than to collapse and embrace her exhaustion, to let sleep overtake her.

Shouts from beyond the hangar door and the sounds of muffled explosions reminded her she wasn't out of the fight yet. Palms against the deck, she gathered her strength and forced herself up. The sharp pain in her ribs and the blaster burns to her shoulder nearly made her left arm collapse beneath her, but she managed to get into a seated position. Grimly, she studied the carnage around her and shuddered at the orange pools of blood. Though she knew the Varanul were genetic abominations bred for one purpose, she never had taken joy in ending a sentient life.

Groaning, she moved away from the gore and cleaned the blood from her blade before slipping it back into its scabbard. The familiar weight on her back comforted her. Edolit was battered and bruised, bleeding from a half dozen wounds and had at least two broken ribs. She had lost her Ambra. Despite all her wounds and the grief she felt at Nian's loss, she allowed herself to feel the elation of relief. The familiar sound of *The Specter's* engines roared loud outside. They were almost home. She'd saved them.

Chapter 31.

C'mon Specter, hold together a little longer.

Uh, Paul? The ship is not sentient.

"No time to explain personification, just help me keep track of these troops!"

A bright flash against the shields in front of the viewport made Paul flinch instinctively. He tried to blink away the bright spots dancing in front of his eyes. When they didn't disappear, he realized his view was blocked by a steady stream of concentrated blaster fire. Vague shapes moved in the haze, but not enough to know what he was seeing. He cursed and checked his shield strength.

[Forward Shield: 68%, Rear Shield: 73%]

Great, they're trying to blind me and have a chance at taking me out. His mind raced as his eyes scanned the console. A switch near the copilot's seat caught his eye. *There, that's the one!*

He leaned over as far as he could without losing control of the ship and flicked the switch. The viewport screen switch to a dull green glow and bright yellow lines appeared, a three-dimensional representation of the hanger outside, based on the ship's sensor readings. A moment later, orange silhouettes of Varanul flashed into view, moving quickly around the hanger, projected behind the outlines of various objects they used for cover.

He smiled and jerked the ship quickly to one side, firing lasers the whole way and melted one of those sources of cover to slag. The orange silhouette of the creature that had been hiding behind it disappeared, either neutralized by his blast or the shrapnel.

"I see you now."

He gave the forward thrusters some power, and the ship lurched deeper into the hangar bay. The viewport cleared, but he kept the sensor display engaged, overlaying the view of the hanger with the outlines created by the computer. As he came around the corner into the main hangar, he targeted one cluster of troopers still standing guard by the entrance Edolit and her team would come from. With a quick series of concentrated blasts, Paul destroyed the barricade that the fire team crouched behind and took most of their numbers out of the fight.

The second fire team guarding the door scattered deeper into the second launch bay before he could bring the ship around. His scanners showed a small cluster inside, behind another barricade, but they were out of his firing range. Edolit would have to deal with them on her own. He ignored them and spun the ship back around towards another hatchway. Varanul and what he assumed to be crewmen of another species were streaming out into the hangar bay. Paul concentrated his fire on the new threats as they scattered around the hanger, splitting his focus.

A few seconds later, Zyp chimed in. ***Omaro reports they have reached the exit hatch and are ready for extraction.***

"About time!" Paul squeezed the trigger and cut down a group of crewman inside another hatchway. The hatch doors became free from their housing and half closed, blocking easy entry from the corridor beyond.

They report two wounded, evacuation will be slow.

"I'll get as close as I can." Paul stopped firing and looked at his tactical readout, using it to guide his counter-thrust back towards the entrance as best he could. He ignored the steadily falling shield value as the dozens of surviving crewmen and

Varanul pelted his shields. As long as he was drawing their fire, they wouldn't be aiming for the wounded. He kept the ship hovering above the deck and cut thrust. He wasn't confident he could get any closer.

"This is the best I can do. Send them a full tactical display and let them know we've got heavy fire."

Done. Lower boarding ramp, they're coming.

With a flick of a switch, the ramp lowered and the chaotic sounds of the hangar bay flooded through the calm of the ship. Shouted commands cut through the blaster fire. He gripped the throttle and stick tightly, trying to keep the ship as steady as possible and ignoring the urge to shy from the steady torrent of concentrated fire. The shield value decreased faster as more crew joined the fight. He evened the shields out with a press of a button.

"Hurry, we've only got a few more seconds!"

***

Private Numoh had expected carnage in the hangar bay, but he was still unprepared for the chaos he was met with as he stormed through the doors. He dove to the side for cover. The guards who had been flanking him got mowed down by strafing fire from the transport and the doors clanked half closed behind them, dislodged from its housing.

Scattered around the hanger, what remained of his security force shot towards the transport ship as it backed towards the entrance to C deck. Battle formations and command structure seemed to have collapsed. The remaining Varanul seemed to be aiming to punch through the shields and damage either the engines or the viewport, depending on their fields of fire.

With a moment's assessment, Numoh knew they wouldn't be able to stop it. Too many of the heavy pulse cannons had been destroyed. He also knew the starfighters were still too far away to make it in time for effective pursuit. Ducking from the chaos, he scanned the undamaged section of the hangar for options. Relief ran through him when he saw one troop transport shuttle was still undamaged. *If I can get to that, I can disappear.*

A flash of indignation coursed through him. His sense of

duty bristled at the thought of abandoning his task. He knew he was going to be sent off to a menial post on the most backwater of worlds if he stayed. At worst, he would be executed, especially the way the battle seemed to be turning. The transport settled beside the entrance and lowered its ramp. Numoh took the chance to run towards his only salvation.

A sudden burst of light caught his attention, and he turned to see the entrance to C deck opening. Edolit waved the other two members of her team forward while she fired back towards a flanking crewman. The hulking Scyllarian helped the armless Grr'alis move quickly up the ramp. Numoh had a clear shot on all of them. Maybe he could redeem himself.

The chitinous Scyllarian turned towards him as he brought up his blaster to fire. He could see from the way it moved that the hulking Scyllarian recognized him. It let out an angry roar that shook Numoh to the core and heaved toward him until Edolit pulled it to a stop with the stern bark of an order.

Private Numoh dropped his weapon and ran towards the troop transport, dropping any aspiration of redemption along with it. Numoh realized how poor of a shot he was. Without a perfect headshot, the rifle would do little but slow down the creature he had tortured. Numoh kept running, not stopping to see if Commander Vyn's orders had kept the Scyllarian from running him down and ripping him apart.

***

Paul turned at the harsh sounds of boots pounding against the deck of the ship. For a moment, the horrible thought of Varanul storming the cockpit and tearing into him with their talons made his heart race. Instead, a huge alien covered in chitin armor burst through the cockpit, oozing blood and covered in burns. It pointed out the viewport with its blaster at one of the gangly gray aliens running away.

"Blast that one if you can, it's the captain." The alien's voice came from two places at once, a chittering noise from its face and a louder translation from its Ambra mounted in its colossal, armored arm.

Before Paul could reply, it disappeared down the hall and helped two others onto the ship. Paul watched anxiously until he saw Edolit stumble through the hatchway. She looked terrible, but relief coursed through him.

"We're all here, let's go," she shouted. She leaned against the inner wall of the ship and punched the hatch controls, closing the ramp. She collapsed to the deck, her back to the wall.

Paul pressed the throttle forward and headed towards the launch bay.

The captain appears to be heading towards that troop transport. Zyp made the outline of the ship flash in his HUD. An icon flashed on the copilot's station next to him, and a stream of laser fire burst into view from above him.

That giant lobster-like alien must be on the dorsal turret, Paul thought as he swung the ship around toward the transport. The gray alien was almost to the ramp of a large transport ship. Blaster fire from *the Specter's* dorsal turret burned holes in the deck all around the lanky creature, tracking its desperate movements closely.

Paul did not know what armament the troop transport had, but he didn't want to find out. He lined up his shot and fired, burning through the rear hull of the vessel. The alien skidded to a stop just before the ramp, and Paul kept firing. Explosions tore the ship apart in a burst of flame as Paul's blasts hit the transport's engines. The blast caught the alien unprepared and sent it tumbling to the deck. It struggled to rise until a quick series of laser blasts from *the Specter's* dorsal cannon caught it in squarely in the chest. Paul cringed at the gory pieces of the creature splattering over the hangar.

Paul aimed the ship towards the twinkling stars at the end of the launch tube and set the throttle to full. He was about to turn on the cloaking device when he saw multiple ships appear on the combat map. The ship's nose outside the viewport disappeared when he flicked the device on, anyway.

Great, the starfighters just got into sensor range.

Cut thrust... now!

Without questioning, Paul cut the throttle to zero and shut the engines off. The speed they had built up in the launch tube sent the ship bursting into the void of space. The chaos of the hangar and the hulking cruiser faded behind them. Paul braced himself, waiting for the cruiser's cannons to tear the ship apart.

The shots never came. Zyp had gotten him to cut thrusters in time to avoid detection by the gunners. They'd made it.

A pair of bright drive plumes caught his attention. The starfighters were close enough to see the glow of their thrusters as they streaked towards their base ship. He resisted the urge to turn and burn hard away from them. He knew they couldn't survive another dogfight, especially with weakened shields. Paul kept the ship drifting forward, hoping their momentum was enough to get them away without detection.

When the starfighters streaked past, their course unchanging, he finally relaxed and collapsed in the seat, exhausted. He'd made it.

"Let's not do that again, Zyp."

I concur. Can we please get out of this hellish star system now?

Paul laughed. "Yes Zyp, I think we can leave now."

Chapter 32.

Paul's skin crawled as *the Specter* drifted away. He knew the remaining starfighters were close. The urge to know where they were ate at him, but he forced himself to keep the cloak engaged. He couldn't help feeling that the ship would be spotted and vaporized at any moment, though he knew the likelihood a pilot could see the shimmer of the ship's cloak field against the backdrop of space without thrusters engaged was slim to none. He'd spent days facing one crisis after another, and now he couldn't shake the feeling. His entire nervous system was overloaded, primed for action and unable to shut down.

According to sensor readings before cloaking, the chance of detection is essentially zero. You should check on the status of the others and take a break from the cockpit. Don't make me give you a sedative again.

Paul was too exhausted to react to Zyp. His legs were stiff from sitting with his tension for hours. The sounds of scrambled movement and muffled groans in the main hold behind him were disorienting. He'd been alone for days, with no noise but the sounds of his own thoughts and Zyp's voice in his head. The noise of other beings on the ship was a welcome change.

"Okay, I'm going to go check on them." He yawned and

stretched, surprised at the aches he felt from tensing his muscles throughout the rescue. He took one last look at the sea of stars and headed to the rear of the ship. As he walked, he ran his hands along the ship's smooth metal as he went; *the Specter* was beginning to feel like home, but he was still trying to get to know it.

Thank you, Specter. As he'd gotten more connected to the ship, it only felt natural to thank it for seeing them through. He wondered if it was a human thing to personify vehicles, or if other species did that too.

Paul found the three aliens clustered around the medical station in the main hold, looking ragged. Edolit was arguing with the larger, crustaceous alien, who seemed to be insisting she let him patch up her wounds. At first glance, she looked like she had received the worst of it until he saw the thin, pink-skinned alien was missing an arm, her shoulder wound grisly and skin hanging loose over her emaciated body.

Edolit noticed him walking into the hold. Her skin pulse a vibrant blue. She smiled, her green eyes twinkling in the bright light of the hold.

"Paul! Good to see you again!" Her voice was ragged, but joyous.

"Zyp says we got away without detection. I thought I'd come check on you," he said, rubbing his hands through his greasy hair and shifting his weight uncomfortably.

The other two aliens spun around. The larger one had a wide grin on his face, or at least Paul thought it was a grin. It was hard to tell what the movement of his facial maxilla meant, but it seemed cheery somehow. The armless one looked weary. Paul walked up and got a closer look at their injuries.

Edolit was holding her left arm close to her side as if she couldn't move it and was covered in a dozen wounds of various shapes and sizes, oozing blue with blood. Her previously vibrant, lilac skin looked dull by comparison, like the color had been drained from her. Ripples of dark red radiated from her wounds in a steady rhythm, showing pain, he assumed.

The large alien had almost as many holes in his chitinous

armor plates. Viscous yellow liquid oozed from the wounds, and scorch marks surrounded them. His wounds were no longer bleeding, but a thin film of gristly flesh was growing over them, his Ambra patching him up. The creature's thin, black eyes drooped beneath the chitin ridges of its face. It was exhausted, too.

Paul's HUD flashed beside the creature. [Omaro: Level 5 Weapons Specialist. Species: Scyllarian. Display bio?].

The small, pink skinned alien was covered in thin, brown bony ridges breaking through her skin, outlining the skeletal edges of her petite frame and extending from the base of her elongated skull. Other than her missing arm, she appeared drained more than wounded and leaned weakly against the wall with a haunted expression.

[Ja'el. Level 4 Pilot. Species: Grr'alis. Display bio?].

Paul closed both HUD display windows with a thought. He was getting more used to working with the Ambra.

"Now that we're safe, can you help me convince her to let me patch her up?" Omaro motioned towards Edolit and crossed his hulking arms. His body language seemed to display annoyance.

Paul turned to Edolit and nodded.

"You look like you've been through hell, you should let him." Paul got an approving nod from the armored alien.

Edolit sighed and sat down on the exam table. Her face pulsed a deep blood red, and she winced. "Fine, Omaro. You win. Let's get this over with."

"Grab me some gelpaks from the kit, Paul." Omaro pointed to a panel in the wall while he started wiping the gelatinous blood from Edolit's shoulder wound with a wet cloth. Paul was surprised at how gingerly the strange creature moved, despite its size.

Paul grabbed a stack of the packets containing the thin, gelatinous matrix of material that reminded him of Edolit's stomach wound from the night they met. His stomach churned as he remembered the grisly sight of her body knitting itself back together. Now that her wounds were cleaned, he could see they weren't healing like before. Without her Ambra, she had to heal the hard way.

Paul glanced down. Fibrous electrodes and metallic bolts of her Ambra still hanging from her forearm. "Do you have another Ambra, to help you heal?"

Edolit coughed and shook her head. She winced as Omaro covered her shoulder wound in the sticky film of the gelpak. "No, I'll be fine until we get back to base."

"She just had to be the hero. It should have been me," Omaro grumbled.

Edolit smiled weakly. "But you make such a good shield. I got us out of there, didn't I?"

"Yeah, and you nearly got yourself killed because of it, too," Omaro said. "At least I blasted that damned Captain Numoh."

Omaro spat out the name like a curse and then turned to Paul and lowered his head. "Thanks for the pickup, kid. We wouldn't have made it without you."

Ja'el chimed in from below them, having slid down to the deck while Omaro patched up Edolit. "Thank you. That was some excellent flying. I didn't think we'd make it out of that one."

"Just trying to help." Paul felt his cheeks burning. He felt out of his league.

"I'm glad you ignored my order to get through the Gate. You did good," Edolit said.

Grief coursed through Paul, hitting him in the gut. The memory of a mushroom cloud breaking through the air above El Paso brought tears to his eyes. "Not good enough. I should have been able to stop all those bombs."

Ja'el cocked her head at him. "I don't think I could manage that, and I've been flying this ship for three standard rotations. No one could have stopped them all."

Edolit nodded, her skin pulsing a bright green. "You've done far more than anyone could have expected of you under the circumstances."

Paul felt a fire inside himself, urging him forward. "I want to do better. Take me with you, there's nothing left for me there, I'm ready to join."

Omaro held out an armored hand, his four digits segmented

like a crab's and covered in ridges. Paul clasped the alien's hand, surprised at the tenderness of its grip.

Edolit beamed at him. "Welcome to the Resistance, Paul."

Chapter 33.

Edolit refused to rest after her wounds were patched up. Medical scans showed she had fractured two ribs, but wasn't in direct danger as long as she didn't take another direct hit. She'd taken a minimum dose of pain medication and locked the rest away in her cabin. She didn't think Ja'el would take too many again, but she didn't want to take the chance. She'd ordered the Grr'alis to take a sedative and rest; the pilot was worn deep to the core and was asleep in her bunk in moments.

Edolit wasn't sure if her friend would ever be the same, but couldn't worry about that now. Omaro was as stubborn as ever, refusing to rest and gorging himself on rations. He was fueling his Ambra's increased caloric needs to heal himself and assured her he would be ready for battle.

Paul was watching Edolit as she worked on her message in the cockpit. He'd agreed warning the people of Earth of the incoming battleship was the best they could do under the circumstances. *The Specter* was out of missiles, and could do little to slow the cruiser down while ten starfighters protected it. The conversation had pained Paul, but he had accepted it. It had only been a few days since everything he had ever assumed about the universe had been shattered; she was proud of how quickly he was embracing it.

Edolit finished her recording and looked back to Paul for approval.

"I don't know if they'll act on it, but it's the best we can do. My planet has never been good at listening to reason."

"No, they haven't, that's why the Gryx seemed prepared to destroy your culture to take the planet. They knew you would be hard to control."

Paul smiled. "We can be pretty obstinate."

"I know, fortunate for me and my crew." Edolit smiled and turned back to the comm station, double checking her settings. She made sure it would send on all frequencies and channels she had uncovered during her time scouting Earth. She'd assured Paul it would be picked up by both military and private receivers alike. He didn't like the idea of the world leaders keeping the public in the dark about their fate. It might cause panic, but she had agreed it was the right thing to do.

"Okay. Data stream ready to send on your mark," she said.

Paul double checked the navigation screen to make sure the coordinates for the Gate were entered and turned off the cloaking field. "Mark."

The sound of Edolit's recording filled the cockpit as Paul engaged the engines. He knew their burn would send starfighters scrambling towards their position. With Zyp's help, he had programmed a route that would take them behind a Jovian moon before the starfighters could intercept. The moon would allow them to make a course correction burn under the moon's sensor shadow and burn hard for the Gate. He checked the sensor feed as the cloaking field dissipated. The ship surged forward under the power of the drive.

"People of Earth, I am Commander Edolit Vyn, of the planet Hylia. I bring you dire warning of imminent danger to your world. Your world has been under assault from a force from the planet Gryx. The Gryx are responsible for the tragedy that consumed the city of El Paso, despite our best efforts to stop their attack. Now their base ship is en route to claim your world for their own." Paul cringed at the mention of El Paso, but kept his focus on the combat map, watching the starfighters change course towards their position.

Edolit continued. "My ship is powerless to stop the advance of this warship ourselves. We are in transit to rally reinforcements to help your world, and will be back in a matter of days. Encoded in this message is a technical analysis of the weaknesses of the Gryx ship. Though their weaponry outmatches yours, perhaps you can defend your world. Regardless, I hope this gives you the chance to get as many of your people to shelter as possible before we return with support. We will not abandon you in your time of need."

When her message was completed, and the tech data sent, Paul shut down the drive and engaged the cloak. He looked down at the combat display and frowned. Most of the starfighters were out of range now, but two seemed to be follow them closely.

"Looks like we picked up two shadows," he said.

Edolit nodded. "We'll lose them when we make our course correction. Did you pick up anything else? Check long range sensor data."

Paul hit a couple of buttons on the console, and the viewport display brought up a representative map of the system. He spotted the cruiser and six of the interceptors en route to Earth and saw another two interceptors had broken away towards their location, moving to join the pair behind them. He also found the angular shape of the gate station, beyond the orbit of Saturn.

"Sensors aren't picking up anything else."

"Good. We stick to the plan and make for the Gate. Prepare for hard burn."

Paul was quiet while he entered the new set of maneuvers. Edolit noted he still cocked his head to listen to Zyp speak. She knew his brain hadn't quite figured out where the voice was coming from yet, and needed to apply some directionality to it. If he stayed with her team, he'd have to work on that. She didn't think he'd end up on her crew, though, at least not completely. He showed too much promise as a pilot to be sent on scouting missions and covert ground strikes. Command would see his performance and put him in a starfighter. The thought of losing him as a team member pained her, but she suspected they'd need all the pilots they could get soon enough.

I wish we could access the network. I need to see what is happening out there. Edolit knew that her flood of the Syndicate materials and her scouting reports would reveal their plans. Would it be enough to motivate The Federation into action, or would they just form an investigative committee while the border planets burned? Next to her, Paul was jittery, anxious to get behind the Jovian moon and shake the starfighters. He was focused on making it through the Gate as fast as they could and bringing back help for his world.

Edolit couldn't help but worry for all the worlds of the border at that moment, alone and without warning. Some would be dead cinders, targeted for resource extraction like the Syndicate seemed to have planned for Earth. They would send others to labor for the Gryx, used to fill Gryx coffers and build their war machine. As Paul engaged the primary drive, she felt it deep in the pit of her stomach. As the dampeners compensated for the inertial forces, the pressure in her stomach lingered. Deep down, Edolit knew the shadow war had become real. She hoped she had gotten the warning out in time to change the outcome.

Chapter 34.

Paul didn't know what to expect from the Gate. He'd tried to get Zyp to explain it, but the number of words he didn't understand in the first sentence alone was enough to make his head spin. However it worked, he'd imagined a glowing vortex of energy harnessed by some technology he couldn't hope to understand.

As the ship approached the Gate, Paul found it was far more unspectacular than he had imagined. In fact, the Gate looked like nothing. From a distance, the Gate was a void, a dark spot in space only visible because of what it blocked from view. The Gate's dark structure blotted out the stars behind it, giving it the appearance of a hole in the fabric of space itself.

"Well, I guess that's why astronomers never saw the Gate with their telescopes," he muttered. When he was younger, conspiracy theories about a dark planet deep at the edge of our solar system had amused him. He'd spent hours on message boards laughing at people convinced a lost planet was responsible for the strange pull of gravity found in the outer reaches of the system. Paul suspected he was now looking at the true source of the strange gravity in the outer system.

As the ship got closer, he saw dark metallic structures with faint lights on their surface dividing the dark void of the Gate into cells over the surface. Roughly the size of a small moon, the Gate was covered in dozens of cells, each the size of a small city. The angular honeycomb of interlocking darkness gave the entire structure the shape that reminded him of a gaming dice.

Each section connects to another node in the Gate system. Zyp answered his silent wonder about the structure.

Does it connect to every world in the civilization? He asked. It still felt weird having a conversation in his head, but he was in awe of the strange structure ahead and didn't want to break the moment with sound yet.

No, each Gate connects to 24 nearby systems, together they create a network that spans the systems of the Federation and the expansion zones.

The clattering of someone coming into the cockpit made him jump.

"Ah, almost to the Gate," Omaro said, stopping to stand next to Paul and looking out the viewport. "I always get the chills when I see them."

"Yeah, it's not what I expected."

The tall alien looked down at Paul and nodded. "You're taking all of this pretty well, all things considered."

Paul shrugged. "I guess part of me always dreamed about being out here and seeing the galaxy. It's enough to keep me from curling up into a ball."

Omaro's maxilla chittered in a distinctive pattern that Zyp displayed as amusement in his HUD. "You know, as strange as all the beings of the galaxy are, that's one thing uniting us all."

"What's that?"

"All sentient beings look up at the same stars and wonder what's out there, and part of them wants to see for themselves. It unites all sentient beings."

The Scyllarian tensed and let out a warbling growl, its dark eyes staring at the Gate. Paul looked out the viewport and frowned.

Didn't we just leave this party? Zyp groaned.

Two large ships were appearing at the edge of a cell of the Gate, cutting through the blackness as if emerging from a pool of water. One was the familiar shape of a *Xyanthin-class* cruiser, like the one he had rescued the crew from. The other was a large, half-dome shape, like a metallic jellyfish. The curved edges of the ship were dotted with weapons blisters and towers, mounted behind armored plating. Nestled in the recessed underside of the ship were dozens of menacing-looking smaller ships attached to the platform bristling with weapons towers.

What's that second ship, Zyp? Paul asked.

A Harrier-class carrier. Most species use them as a mobile ground assault platform. Would you like me to display its stats?

Not now.

"Ka'ilk! Those are Gryx reinforcements." He moved to the console and checked the computer readout. "It will take them a long time to get to the planet but if we can't get back with reinforcements then..."

"Then my world is lost."

He nodded. "I'll go wake the Commander. Keep our heading, but do nothing to alert their sensors."

The firm hand of the Scyllarian patted his shoulder as the alien left the cockpit, a gesture Paul decided was intended to be reassuring. Paul was left alone, staring out at the assault force picking up speed as it moved away from the Gate.

***

Edolit burst onto the bridge and settled into the copilot's chair.

"Is there anything we can do?" Paul looked at her pleadingly.

She shook her head. "Not with what we've got left on *the Specter*. We need to get through the Gate and bring back reinforcements. We can make it back in time to help the fight for your world."

She started programming the navigational computer for a series of short micro-thruster bursts. Paul watched her, his mind racing for another option. He wasn't ready to run away yet, but there was little he could do, and he knew it. Within moments of revealing themselves, there would be a dozen starfighters scrambling towards them. He suspected that if they somehow dealt with the starfighters and stayed out of range of the cruisers' point defense cannons, the troop transports would join the fray.

The ships mounted on the *Harrier-class* carrier looked clunkier than the sleek starfighters, but he could tell they were heavily armored and clearly sported a rotating laser cannon similar to *the Specter's*. While he was confident he could out-fly a handful of them, an entire wing of them would be too many to handle. He'd inflict minimal damage before being vaporized, and his death wouldn't change the outcome for Earth.

Resigned, he nodded and kept his eyes locked on the slow-moving ships. Two pairs of starfighters left the launch bay of the cruiser simultaneously, swooping out both sides of the ship's hangar in unison and looping around to take up escort positions on either side of the two cruisers. A moment later, four more fighters launched and split into escort positions in vectors above and below the troop transport carrier.

Edolit studied their movements. "They're being cautious. Whoever is in command here is much more competent than Captain Numoh was. See here, they're setting up a fighter screen to protect as many vectors as they can. Command has alerted them to our possible presence. We couldn't get off more than a couple missiles before they were on top of us, even if we had more in the tubes."

"So let's get to the Gate."

With each burst of the micro-thrusters, Paul held his breath, expecting the starfighters to spot them. Even under direct sensor scans, the small bursts of vented gases were virtually impossible to detect on scanners, Edolit assured him. He couldn't shake his feeling of imminent doom. It didn't help they had to cut speed to approach the Gate because of something about the gravity field he didn't understand. The result was a painfully slow approach as the Gryx ships pulled away and picked up speed.

After what seemed like hours, the Gate was filling the viewport as the autopilot nudged the ship towards a particular cell of the strange honeycomb structure with precise bursts. Closer now, Paul could see that the surface of each cell rippled like a murky wave of pure dark energy. He felt a tinge of panic, his instinctual lizard-brain afraid of the dark unknown.

Paul nearly screamed when a dozen points of light burst through the darkness ahead of them. The points expanded over the surface of the Gate in rippling waves of energy, and from origin points metallic objects burst into the space around them like metallic fingers reaching from the blackness.

"Pull up!," Edolit yelled as a bright point appeared in the rippling dark directly ahead of *the Specter*.

Paul's stomach lurched as the main drive kicked on as he engaged thrust and pulled on the controls, narrowly avoided the hull of the large ship emerging from the Gate. Ships emerged in the space ahead of them as they flew parallel to the rippling edge of hyperspace. Some were small transports similar in design to *the Specter*, but most were cruisers of various shapes and sizes.

"That's the *Adamant*," Edolit said, her voice full of excitement as she pointed to the largest ship emerging from the rippling black. "De-cloak, now!"

Paul switched off the cloak and set them into a course alongside the ship Edolit had pointed out. The combat display filled with a dozen ships surrounding them. The Gryx cruisers still pulled away from the Gate, their shields already glowing as the new arrivals sent streams of laser fire toward them.

"Commander Vyn of *the Specter* to *Adamant*. Good to see you," Edolit said into the comm.

A moment later, an authoritative voice answered. "Commander, this is *Adamant* actual. Sorry we couldn't get here sooner. That message of yours sure stirred things up. Looks like the Gryx reinforcements beat us here."

"General Thriss, I'm glad you're here. Where do you need us?" Edolit said.

"Get to the hanger, your team has done their part. Now let us do ours."

Paul paled and looked to Edolit. He wasn't ready to be out of the fight. Not until he knew his world was safe. He met her eyes and shook his head, pointing to the new targets appearing around the Gryx ships as they launched their starfighters and troop transports. He wasn't going anywhere.

"Negative, *Adamant,* we've got a pilot from Earth now. We'll see this one through," she said into the comm, with an approving nod towards Paul.

"Understood. Help keep transports and bombers away from the cruisers. I'll redirect a flight group to provide cover. Good hunting. *Adamant out.*"

Edolit hit a switch on her console, switching control of the forward guns to her station. "You fly, Omaro and I will shoot."

Edolit switched over to the ship's comm. "Omaro, strap in Ja'el, and get on the dorsal gun, we're going in. Concentrate on the transports and bombers, but keep those starfighters off our tail."

Paul veered *the Specter* towards the rapidly advancing swarm of enemy fighters and transports and set shields to double front. He felt a calm certainty wash over him as he angled towards a cluster of transports. This was where he belonged.

Chapter 35.

Paul had a hard time processing the battle as it unfolded around *the Specter*. His previous encounters in space were orderly compared to the swirling chaos of a full-scale battle. Caught by surprise, the Gryx ships reacted like cornered predators, flailing at the newcomers with frenzied desperation. Cut off from escape through the Gate, and with no time to charge up their FTL drives, the Gryx committed everything they could towards trying to break the blockade. Paul got the impression that they would have sent out their maintenance shuttles if they had a blaster strapped to them.

Within moments, three dozen troop transports dropped from their docking clamps beneath their carrier ship, and scattered towards the Resistance cruisers in chaotic flight groups. Starfighters and bombers streamed from the dual hangers of the Gryx cruiser as it came about, trying to angle its heavily armored bow toward the newcomers.

The *Adamant* delivered devastating broadside attacks, flanking the lumbering Gryx cruiser before it could come about. Resistance starfighters streamed from launch tubes and hangers on the four capital vessels, and the battle was raging. The tactical screen was a swirling mess of data that Paul couldn't make sense of. He regretted his decision to join the battle until Edolit began acting like the commander he needed.

"Break towards those transports, and keep us away from our

frigates' fields of fire," she ordered, pointing toward the Gryx troop carrier. Paul saw the ship was rotating on its axis, bringing more of its cannons to bear on two smaller Resistance frigates tearing into its hull from beneath with concentrated cannon fire.

Paul set course for the cluster of troop transports heading toward a Resistance gunship, a small, needle-like ship moving toward the Gryx cruiser. The gunship's shields were already beginning to glow from the transports' concentrated laser fire. He didn't know if the swift vessels were loaded with troops or not, but they were certainly well armed.

"Omaro, concentrate on the lead transport. I'll dissuade the others," she growled into the comm.

"Copy, Commander."

A steady stream of fire poured into the lead ship from *the Specter*'s dorsal cannon, while Edolit sent short bursts dancing between the other three ships in the group. Her calm demeanor kept Paul from breaking as defensive fire from the transports' rotating cannons began splashing against the forward shields.

With grim efficiency, Edolit made the crosshairs dance across the viewscreen, rotating the forward turret to match the transport's motion as they bobbed and weaved, trying to complete their bombing runs. The lead ship broke apart under Omaro's concentrated fire, seriously damaging its distracted squad mates in the rapidly expanding cloud of debris. The remaining transports wavered, damaged by shrapnel and tumbling out of control into the gunship's field of fire. The gunship mopped them up with precise blasts.

Before Paul could ask for more direction, Edolit pointed out another group on the combat map. "Okay, same thing on this flight group."

Paul spun the ship towards the targets, noticing the shaking in his hands subsiding. He was no longer alone, reacting to situations by instinct alone; he had help. Edolit guided them, and Omaro made them more deadly. Paul was more comfortable knowing all he had to do was keep flying.

***

As he walked down the ramp of *The Specter* onto the flight deck behind Edolit, Paul noticed the mood aboard the *Adamant* was more grim than he expected for the victors of a battle. He assumed the hanger would be full of elated starfighter pilots jumping from their cockpits and hugging each other, surrounded by techs and crewman celebrating the outcome of the battle.

You've seen too many movies, Zyp scoffed at him.

Instead of celebration, Paul watched a somber crowd gathering in front of a screen with scrolling text. Zyp translated the alien script for him without comment, and Paul got a glimpse of the news feed. Damage reports, names of the wounded and the dead, names of ships lost, and locations of life pod recovery in process. His face burned as the reality of war set in.

Outnumbered and cut off from escaping through the Gate, the Gryx had lashed out, attacking viciously to attempt to break through. When breaking the blockade had proved hopeless, the Gryx settled for causing as much damage as possible. The Resistance frigate *Kaddi* had been destroyed, along with a transports ship and half a squadron of starfighters. Victory had been costly.

Edolit limped through the hanger, past starfighters marred by carbon scouring and emitting showers of sparks onto the techs rushed to repair damage. She led him towards the corridor at the end of the hanger, her skin pulsing a plethora of clashing colors. She caught him staring, trying to figure out the conflicting emotions pulsing across her skin.

"We've seen this war coming for years, but this is the first proper battle we've seen. Most of them always hoped we could stop it." Her voice was weak, strained as much by her injuries as the weight of the moment. "I always knew it would come to this, though. The signs have been there for years."

"Is this happening everywhere?"

"That's what we're going to find out."

***

Edolit led Paul through the winding corridors to the bridge. Paul tried his best to keep from staring, but couldn't quite help himself. The ship was filled with at least a dozen species of aliens of all shapes and sizes, bustling about in the aftermath of battle. He recognized members of the same species as *the Specter's* crew. Scyllarians with their chitin plate armor and crustacean-like appearance, and the small, thin Grr'alis with a wide array of colorful skin colors and bony ridges. He even saw the occasional member of Edolit's species, their lilac skin rippling with color as they stormed past him.

Among them were fearsome creatures with wide, flat heads bristling with gnarled fangs, covered in matted fur. Reptilian humanoids covered in iridescent scales watched him pass with curiosity, segmented red eyes unblinking. Insectoid creatures gathered in groups, their vestigial wings flapping uselessly as they chittered excitedly.

He'd overcome most of his shock by the time they made it to the bridge and he was eternally grateful to have been partially desensitized before he saw General Thriss. The General towered over the bridge, a hulking creature with blood red skin and folded wings draped along its back. Bulging muscles rippled beneath its crisp, black uniform and its bright blue eyes glowered at an array of screens. A dozen curved horns spiraled around its skull, protecting it like a gruesome warrior's helmet.

Edolit stopped in front of the creature and saluted.

"At ease, Commander Vyn, I'm glad to see you made it." General Thriss said in a deep, booming voice. He looked her up and down. The creature's face was serene, out of place against the alien's devilish appearance. "It appears you should have been to the med bay before reporting in."

"I'm okay, General. I'm eager to hear what's been happening." She hesitated and shifted uncomfortably. "I'm also prepared to face the consequences of my actions."

"Consequences?" The general cocked his head. "Do you deserve a reprimand I'm not aware of?"

"I disobeyed a direct order by involving this human in my mission," Edolit said. Paul shook as the creature turned to look at him with narrowed eyes. "I also leaked sensitive information to the quantum network."

"Yes, yes. And were I in your boots, I would have done the same. I'm prepared to defend you to the Council, but it won't come to that. I believe they will be too busy at the moment."

"What has happened?"

"War. Your leak caught the Gryx and their criminal Syndicate unprepared. We protected as many worlds as we could with our limited resources while they scrambled to react. We trapped many of their expeditionary forces as we did here, but we lost more systems than we saved." The General paused and brought up a map on the screen. It looked wildly different from the map Edolit had shown Paul before. At a glance, he could see segmented territories and fronts already forming.

"The more competent of their commanders consolidated forces and abandoned the least important targets to overtake more strategic positions. Unfortunately, their plans went far deeper than a power grab on the border worlds, it had roots deep in the core worlds. The Federation's entire Sixth Fleet defected under direct command of Admiral Hya. All other fleets experienced some level of sabotage, including assassination of many higher-level officers and loss of multiple capital ships. The Federation itself is fractured, with dozens of core worlds joining the Gryx and remaining fleets scrambling to react. The conflict is already spreading into a chaotic civil war."

Edolit shrank down at this news, and Paul cringed. He knew little about Edolit, but he knew enough to be sure that she'd never forgive herself for starting such a conflict.

General Thriss stood tall and placed a gigantic hand on her shoulder. "Commander Vyn, this war has been brewing for a long time. Do not blame yourself. By forcing their hand before they were ready, you've given us a chance for our civilization to survive." He leveled his eyes at Paul. "And you... you've reminded us there are fighters hidden among the beings we save."

Paul gulped and found the courage to speak. "May I join the flight group sent to intercept the *Wildfire*? I don't know if I can sleep until I know Earth is safe."

The general smiled down at him. "There is no need. Earth has already scared off the Gryx cruiser on its own. *Wildfire* engaged its FTL drive after Earth launched ballistic missiles towards it. Our ships tracked it exiting the system, soon after we engaged the Gryx reinforcements. It will take months for the cruiser to reach another star system without use of the Gate."

Relief swept through Paul. It was over. He'd finally come through.

"Thank you, General." Paul could feel tears welling up in his eyes, and he silently asked Zyp to keep them from flowing. The Ambra complied without comment, though Paul expected he'd get some grief for it later. "I would still like to join the Resistance, if you'll have me."

The general patted his shoulder. Paul was surprised at how gentle the creature's touch was, though its hand dwarfed his chest. "We'll worry about that later. Now, report to med bay and get some rest, both of you. That's an order. Tomorrow, we have a war to win."

***

MESSAGE FROM THE AUTHOR:

Thank you for reading THE SPECTER RISING. I've had a lot of fun working on this novel over the past few months and I hope you enjoyed it. If you've got two minutes, I would sincerely appreciate it if you would take the time to post a review. Not only does this help small time authors like me get some help with getting their work in front of new reader's eyes, but it would be a great way to help me improve my stories. This book was my first novel, and though I learned a lot, I still know that I have a ton to learn.

Love something I'm doing in particular? Let me know, so I know what I'm doing right! Hate something, or find some wild mistakes? Let me know, so I do better next time around (or can fix it). Feedback will help me create better books.

Thank you again.

Until next time,

James Aspen

jamesaspenauthor@gmail.com

Visit my website for updates on my current writing projects and to sign up for my newsletter:

www.jamesaspenwrites.com